GEORGE ELLIOTT was born in London, Ontario, in 1923. He attended the University of Toronto, where he edited the student newspaper, *The Varsity*. When the Second World War broke out, his poor eyesight prevented his military service, and he became editor of the *Strathroy Age-Dispatch*, while acting as Strathroy correspondent for the *London Free Press*. He later became a reporter and city editor with the *Timmins Daily Press*, and local correspondent for the *Toronto Daily Star*. His career in journalism preceded an even more successful career as an advertising executive.

In 1962, he published his first work of fiction, *The Kissing Man*. He uses the southwestern Ontario world of his childhood as the setting of eleven connected short stories that examine the continuing communal traditions among three generations of characters.

George Elliott died in Île d'Orléans, Quebec, in 1996.

George Elliott

THE KISSING MAN

With an Afterword by Bonnie Burnard

This book was first published by the Macmillan Company of Canada in 1962

New Canadian Library edition 1998

Canadian Cataloguing in Publication Data

Elliott, George, 1923 –
The kissing man

(New Canadian library)
ISBN 0-7710-3465-2

I. Title.   II. Series.

PS8509.L55K5   1998   C813'.54   C98-930426-4
PR9199.3.E55K5   1998

We acknowledge the financial support of the Government of
Canada through the Book Publishing Industry Development
Program for our publishing activities. We further acknowledge
the support given by the Canada Council for the Arts and by
the Ontario Arts Council for our publishing program.

Typesetting by M&S, Toronto

Printed and bound in Canada

McClelland & Stewart Inc.
The Canadian Publishers
481 University Avenue
Toronto, Ontario
M5G 2E9

1 2 3 4 5   02 01 00 99 98

But when I speak of the family, I have in mind a bond which embraces . . . a piety towards the dead, however obscure, and a solicitude for the unborn, however remote.

Notes towards the Definition of Culture
by T. S. ELIOT

Contents

ONE

An act of piety

THE LITTLE ROAN bull lunged back and forth along the fence that kept him in the barn-yard. Dried dung scales rattled on his flanks and tail. His ribs heaved in and out, stretching and rippling his rough winter hide. The wet wind from the south brought him the smell of cows plodding through the spring mud, back the lane to pasture. He lunged and snorted back and forth.

The creek foamed and flooded along the low places of the farm, past the barn, beside the garden, undermining the elm roots, foaming to a tan colour under the plank bridge. The creek was high and muddy, gurgling along its banks, pouring on like a river for as long as it could.

Tessie watched, standing on the cement stoop at the back of the house. Growing and urgent, she thought. The bull and the creek. She looked to the east and named off the neighbours: the Dunlops, the Whartons, the Watsons, the MacDonalds, the Thompsons, the Sobels, the Palsons, the Framinghams, and then the town. She looked to the west and saw her father-in-law's barn and the Menders' place, and felt the lake beyond.

She heard her two sons in the kitchen, clattering with the wash basin, pumping water. She turned to go in and, again, received the little shock of surprise: this was her house, hers and Mayhew's. They built it together. They came when Mayhew was stumping and slashing a few acres by the road.

How quickly she had become a woman. She remembered arriving in the township seven years ago. She was nineteen and she wore her auburn hair piled thickly on top of her head. She was proud and had lots of energy and wanted more than anything to be a woman. She practised keeping her lips firmly compressed then. She had been afraid she would have been "left out" in the quiet life of her father's store back on the Dundas highway.

She had come alone to teach in the township school. A Lewis man met her. He asked bluntly, with no hint of feeling in his voice (all the Lewis people were like that), asked her if she thought she was strong enough to work and live in this part of the country.

"Whichever kind of strength you mean, Mister MacDonald, I have it. My kind of strength gives me the strength I expect a teacher needs here."

Each year, as she met the members of the school board, her statement of strength (she thought of it that way) was repeated.

Now, as she looked at the bull and the creek, she was proud of her strength, that it kept her here while Mayhew got up the courage to ask her to marry him, that it kept her going on their hundred acres.

It was a good way to start the day, she thought, really a good way to start the spring, for it was spring and it was the season that mattered.

In the cow-stable window, she saw the light of the lantern being turned down to a dull orange and then out. When its orange glow stopped, she was aware of the light of dawn. She went inside to set the breakfast.

When Mayhew came in, the boys were sitting at the table, waiting. Mayhew looked at Tessie for a moment. When she

saw his face that way she smiled. He knows what's going on.
He knows.

The tea was scalding and strong. The fried potatoes were
hot. The porridge was thick and sweetened. The boys yawned
and rubbed their eyes. They wanted to finish breakfast
quickly and get off to school.

Mayhew stopped eating and turned his chair round so he
could see out the window. "I thought I heard a rig of some
kind," he said.

The family stopped eating and looked out the window
facing the road. Yes, there was the sound of horses' feet on the
wooden planks of the bridge. It sounded like a heavy rig. The
dog barked as the heavily loaded wagon came up the rise in
the road by the big basswood tree.

"Why, it's somebody moving, I believe," Tessie said. "I
wonder who it could be."

Mayhew wondered too, because he knew that all the good
lots along the lake range were occupied from the boundary
north as far as the little islands. He saw there was a man and
his wife and two children in the family on the wagon. The
team of Clydes looked old and weary.

"Well now, finish your breakfast. We'll know in time.
If they're to be neighbours, let's hope they're good ones,"
he said.

That was Tessie's first glimpse of the Irish.

When the children came home from school that afternoon, Tessie and Mayhew learned the names of the new-
comers and where they were from. It was an Irish family from
an old township down East. They came to settle on the base
line because the land that was allotted to them down East was
wind-blown and not good for summer fallow or potatoes.

"Irish!" Tessie whispered to herself.

It was the following Sunday when they got their first close
look at the new family. Turning sedately and a little stiffly,

Tessie watched them come in the river church and sit in a pew near the back, away from the Quebec heater. They were poorly dressed but that was no matter. He was clean-shaven which was unusual for a man in that part of the country. She was a plodding sort and there seemed to be no spirit in her face.

After the service, the new family was greeted, not eagerly, not coldly, and Tessie got a close look at the man and the thing on his neck. She said nothing, showed no sign, but the thought of being the closest neighbour was cruel.

In the democrat on the way home, she remained silent. The children squirmed happily in the back. The horse jogged at its own pace. Mayhew watched his township flow by him.

Alone in the kitchen, Tessie said, "You saw it?"

M "Yes, I saw it."

T "What do you intend to do about it?"

M "What can I do?"

T "You can get them out of here. Back where they came from."

M "Me?"

T "Well, something's got to be done."

He said nothing and she pressed her lips together.

T "And you've got to do something before nine o'clock tomorrow morning or you'll teach the children their lessons yourself. They'll not set foot in that school for one minute as long as those children are allowed to go."

M "I could talk to Mister Framingham, I guess."

T "I should hope so."

"But, Mayhew, there's no lump on the children's necks. Surely if it spreads they'd've gotten it by now." Mr. Framingham was uncomfortable because he sympathized with Mayhew and agreed with him. The Irish family should somehow have been kept out. But he knew they had settled in, their claim to the land was good, their down payment had been accepted, the title was theirs, clear and free.

"So I'm to go back to Missis Salkald and tell her it doesn't spread."

Mr. Framingham said nothing.

"And I suppose you expect to receive the rest of my quarterly payments towards the school? When I won't have any children in it?"

"You know how I feel, Mayhew. Don't ask questions like that."

"Maybe iodine would work."

"Yes, maybe iodine would work."

"But it burns. I can't see the children getting it painted on them every school day."

"Have you any iodine at home?"

"I'll get some."

When he got home, he found Tessie was wearing a band of unbleached cotton round her throat. It gave her the dignity of an old woman, he thought at first, then sighed when he saw what it was for.

"Do you think that will do any good?"

She didn't answer.

"I talked to Mister Framingham."

"What did he say?"

"He said iodine might help."

He was sorry for her that she had to press her lips together that way, and a little ashamed that this had happened to him.

The next morning, after breakfast, the boys lined up solemnly by the kitchen table. Tessie sat with the bottle of iodine in her hand. Each one stepped up to her. She painted the iodine on their throats until a little would trickle down into the hollow of the chest bone.

In the school yard, before the nine o'clock bell was rung, the Salkald kids showed their throats proudly. The Irish children sat alone on the school steps, waiting for the teacher.

Proud Tessie lay dying inside. Honey decided he didn't want to know how to prevent his grandmother from dying. His heart was full of sorrow for the world, that had to bear unexpected dying like this, consuming pain like this; and his heart was full of a terrible fear. Although her dying like this did not mean he was to do an act of sorrow. Her world had been more relentless than his and she had survived for eighty-four years. Actually, "gone to her reward" would be a good way to put it, after it's all over.

Her dying called for something he couldn't explain. While she was alive, this was the Salkald farm. While she was alive, this was the Salkald family.

So while she was dying, the farm clung to him. Walking from the house to the barn, he passed close by the clump of tiger lilies that caressed his overalls. The white roses, wind-blown, and getting ready to die too, glowed a little in the evening darkness. The cedar clump outside the horse-stable door touched Honey's shoulders gently as he passed.

The familiar bulk of the barn was there, on the left. There was no moon to lighten the sky and outline the barn, but Honey's awareness of it was everything he knew about it: the clay gangway, the big granary, the straw mows, the fir silo, the horse stable, the passage-ways, the cow stables, the pig sties, the well, the cement horse trough.

The small cement rectangle in the heart of the barn's big bulk reminded him of his grandmother's spare, brisk figure by bright sunlight as she filled pails with water from the horse trough: burning August sun baking the clean clay, and Grandma, small figure in blue, going from the trough to the hen house and back.

Back behind the barn, Honey lifted himself up onto the rail fence with familiar ease. If he turned his head slightly to the right, he would see the patch of light from the oil lamp in his grandmother's window. If he turned his head slightly to the left, he knew the Salkald farm was there: the stooked wheat, barley just cut, whispering oats, the summer fallow, the brown-green tasselled corn.

So he waited. Proud Tessie lay dying inside, and far out to the south-east the harvest moon was getting ready to be born. The warmth of the day's sun seemed to be still in the cedar rail under his hands.

Alone there on the fence back of the barn, knowing the neighbours' farms were silent and real in the darkness where land and sky met, Honey held his breath. This would be like crouching over a deep well, waiting for the water to settle so he could see his reflection.

Memories flowed through him, memories of his grand-mother moving through the activities of her time that put the breath of reality into this land and these people to make them the Salkald farm and the Salkald family.

He sat this way until the night breeze came over the land. Turning his head, he saw the square of light fade from steady yellow to faltering orange, a glow, then suddenly out.

He thought first of the white roses and knew they wouldn't have that glow in them now. He put his hands on the cedar rail to let himself down. The heat of the day had gone. As he walked by it, the barn was a cold bulk. In the door of the woodshed at the back of the house, he turned. The first severe crescent of what was to be the harvest moon appeared in the black distance over the poplars on the second concession: a cold birth, a travel across the sky, a warm slow dying.

In the kitchen, his mother and aunt sat quiet-faced but not relaxed. They watched as he opened the door to his grand-mother's bedroom. He left it open so the light from the kitchen shone in. He saw someone had wrapped a silk scarf round her head and under the jutting chin.

But she didn't have on her black velvet throat band. She seemed old, weak and without defences. Honey turned out of the room to speak to his mother about it, but unexpectedly, as he closed the door quietly, he knew he would say nothing to her, for fear she didn't know the meaning of the narrow band of black either.

Honey wondered what it was that made a farm belong to someone in particular. As he got into bed, he knew that, early next morning, the dew would lash across his boot tops as he went for the cows, but the farm would be barren and exposed. He wouldn't be able to stop for that secret look at the barn, the biggest in the county, built by his grandfather, Mayhew, and he himself had helped to reshingle the north side of the roof.

They opened the upper half of the coffin at the funeral. Honey didn't get up from his pew and file past with the others. He watched as they wheeled old Mrs. Palson in her wheel-chair up to the coffin. Honey was close enough to the front that he could sit up straight in the pew, lean sideways a little, and see that proud Tessie was wearing her black velvet throat band. No one else had even thought of it.

<u>Naturally, they buried Tessie beside Mayhew in the Anglican graveyard by the lake.</u> The following Sunday, Honey planted grass seed on the new mound of sandy earth. He raked the plot neatly first, then scattered the seed evenly and patted it in firmly with his hands. When he got up off his knees, his forehead dripped perspiration. The sun penetrated him. He leaned the rake against Mayhew's tombstone, then looked at the old mound with the new one beside it.

Well, Mayhew, dead these nine years now. And washed a little at a time by nine spring floods from the churchyard to the creek, from the creek to the river, from the river to Lake Huron.

You were like a kind of Bible patriarch to us kids. For Tessie, you were a husband to look up to as an able provider and helpmate, I guess she'd've said. To Mother and her sisters and Uncle Dan, you were a father to respect, to fear and to be impatient with; and for us kids, you were a grandfather to love and to be in awe of for living so long and healthily.

You were six feet three inches tall, your body a perfect, down-pointing wedge. Your pointed beard and cropped moustache were the marks of authority and wisdom.

You were sick for a few days, but not too sick. The day before, not that she really knew, Tessie asked the minister to call. He did and you sent him away.

"Oh, don't bother," you said. "I've got a religion better than what you offer." Then you died.

I didn't go to your funeral. I didn't want to see you in the coffin on trestles in the parlour. I didn't want to see the aunts crying in sorrow. Now I wish I'd been there.

Uncle Dan recited "Thanatopsis," the way you said he was to. Then they put the coffin in a black sleigh-hearse drawn by four black horses with black tassels on the harness. I close my eyes now and see those dabs of jet jiggling down the fourth concession between the high-banked snows – out west towards a final grey Lake Huron sky.

I guess for eighty years you held up this flat front of hard work, raising a family, being a good farmer, getting the respect of the community, growing old with massive dignity, being a Christian.

But why didn't you pretend to die, as well as live, like one? It's what all the other county pioneers did. But you, you never let God know you were coming at all, never suggested for a minute it had been a pretty good life. You said you had a religion of your own.

Then Honey wondered what it would have been like if he had never heard what his grandfather Mayhew had said to the minister. He wondered what it would have been like if Uncle Dan had not recited "Thanatopsis."

By now, you would be nothing more than the memory of an old man, a swell old man, Mother's father, a big man in the county, whose farm was our summer home in childhood. Nothing more than a man who caught two cattle swindlers by chasing after the train in his horse and buggy. By now the memories would be the fuzzy kind like that.

Honey knew he had to remember all he could about Mayhew and Tessie, his grandparents. He would have to ask Uncle Dan and his mother and the aunts, because now he knew the truth of life and the truth of death were not the same.

So there in the warm sand, by the old grave and the new grave, Honey remembered, and one by one the memories came to him and took convincing shapes.

You took me in the horse and buggy to a barn three miles from home and said, "I hewed and squared all the timbers for this barn. Go in and climb up on the beams. Look carefully. You won't find a single mark of the broad axe. You'd think the timbers all came from the mill." So you told a grandchild from town you were the best man in the county with the broad axe and the adze when it came to building a barn. You never said it, but what you meant was that barns are necessary, and men to build good ones are necessary and worth something.

You drilled the deepest well in the county and got an underground artesian flow. Later, the neighbours, who had shallow surface wells, lined up in the stable yard with their wagons full of milk cans when their wells dried up. You knew about permanence the day you moved onto your own property.

You worked hard and felt that all the things you did were essential, so you created your own comforts that were like bowing to the strength of the land. You were very much like a Christian, but you were Mayhew Salkald first.

Here I am, Honey thought, almost a man and all the days

of the Salkald farm are in me. That is what Mayhew means to me, and really, all my days are yet to come.

The one breathless note of the cicadas swam in the air, never ending, out of the cedars. It burst in on Honey's ears as he took the rake to the tool shed. It was like some strange machine concealed in the cool undergrowth, suddenly running empty, like a threshing machine, whining for replenishment. Honey thought this in the tool shed and didn't want it to happen. His head ached with the heat. It was a long time since lunch. His head, he thought, must be aching because he hadn't had much to eat so far today.

As he walked down the sandy pathway through the headstones, by the little church, across the foot-bridge and through the gate, he saw that old Mrs. Palson had been watching him in the cemetery. It's going to happen now.

Old Mrs. Palson was in her summer kitchen, leaning forward in her wheel-chair so she could see out the window. She rapped the window sharply with her thimble to make him look over at her.

Knowing what was to come, Honey's head spun. The heat seemed dizzying. He was going to find out about Tessie now.

It was past chore time when he left the Palson house and started the quiet walk east along the fourth concession. Behind him, the sun had taken itself under the horizon of the lake. On both sides and ahead, the sky reflected the dying reds and oranges. Ahead was the home farm. The new shingles on the north side of the barn roof caught the sun's last light and the roof seemed silvery metal. It was familiar and good. Honey's mind was full, spinning and weary. He knew enough, now, about Tessie to make the old truth fresh and almost complete.

Honey reached the gate to the farm. The cows were in the yard, waiting. His mother stood at the doorway, watching for him. The milk pails at the cow-stable door held the last light of the day. They were turned upside down, waiting to be righted and used.

The past was in him, never to be forgotten nor ignored. But he didn't know whether he was to forgive. He wanted only to keep what was good and pass it on.

TWO

When Jacob Fletcher was a boy

As well as being a discreet man, Doctor Fletcher was a Bible reader. He could give you about all of Ecclesiastes by heart, if he had a mind to, with a private smile on his face while he was doing it. That smile was there when he told the girl she was going to bear twins.

The girl cried in a helpless way over the idea of twins. When she got around to thinking about what else the doctor said, she didn't know what he was talking about. The nurse didn't either. The doctor touched the girl on her arm to comfort her and left the room, still smiling.

He found the secretary of the Children's Aid waiting for him in the little sitting-room downstairs. "You'll be getting a fine pair of boys in a few days now," the doctor said confidently.

"Twins. We've never had twins before. I suppose the city orphanage has, though."

"I guess you'll have to think up names for them. The girl doesn't want to see them or have anything to do with them," the doctor said.

"It would be good to give them names from the father's family. That'd teach them a lesson," the secretary of the Children's Aid said.

"Here, you listen to me." The doctor's voice was sharp. "Their names don't matter at all. Don't matter at all. Why don't you name them Jacob and Esau? Good Bible names, Jacob and Esau. And there's bound to be trouble between them before they're very old."

"Yes, yes," the secretary shrugged. "Jacob and Esau, if they are boys."

"They'll be boys," the doctor said.

The years went by. Doctor Fletcher kept on delivering babies. The secretary of the Aid got old. Jacob and Esau, for they were boys as the doctor had promised, grew up in the orphanage in the city.

Esau developed a nervous affliction in the orphanage as he came on to adolescence. Jacob was shy and didn't talk or play much with anybody but Esau.

Shy Jacob and nervous Esau came back to the town where they were born. They had to, because there came the day of their sixteenth birthday and the people at the orphanage in the city and the people at the Aid in town had no alternative. And there was a wedding going on in the Anglican church the day the twins, Jacob and Esau, came back to the town where they were born.

Esau remembered that day. One minute, the secretary of the Aid, shaking from palsy now, was telling Jacob and Esau in his old voice to mind and not get in any trouble and to call on the Aid if they ever needed help; and the next minute the door closed and they were out in the June day with the Anglican bell one-noting it unevenly over the ceremony below.

The twins walked away from the Aid office towards the sound of the bell. As they turned onto the side street where the church was they heard the organist matching each bong on the bell with a solemn chord. Esau saw some people he knew from the city on their way to the church. He kept his head down so they wouldn't have to speak to him if they didn't want to.

The twins went past the church and turned onto a wide oak-lined street running parallel to Main. They walked on slowly towards the centre of town, under the oaks, along this street, then across a short side street, then along another where the oaks shadowed both sidewalks. All the time they walked slowly, two steps for each lonely bong of the bell, avoiding the tar-filled cracks in the sidewalk with their toes.

They talked to no one. No one saw them on their slow walk to the lonely bell. The peace of the town came on Jacob and he walked gratefully in the shade of the oaks. Esau walked alertly, watching the road ahead and looking behind him every block.

There was an old carriage shed behind the Queen's Hotel. The windows were broken and the double doors hung askew and the shingles had started the damp rot. The floor was rough field stones with the cement crumbling away and it was always damp. When it rained the water dripped through the shingles on the straw and the straw had a dying, old smell after. The shed was no good for carriages or horses any more, so the twins, Jacob and Esau, went there.

The Kennedys – that's Gerry's father and mother, they owned the Queen's – let them stay. What else could they have done? The twins were quiet and clean-talking as far as anybody knew. They were as presentable as, say, big Audie Seaton, the handy man.

Esau thought the carriage shed was first rate because, before he got free of the Aid, he wanted most to get away from people and to be alone and to do what he wanted to do or do nothing and not worry about it. He thought the loft was a nifty place to sleep and there was an old tack trunk for him and one for Jacob to keep their belongings in: copper-toed boots, toques, the heads of their sucker spears, an old gill net, a gallon jug, a black lunch pail, the magnifying glass.

The carriage shed didn't matter to Jacob. The idea of being alone with Esau and away from the orphanage was all right, but within a few weeks it became obvious there would never be enough odd jobs for both boys to do, so Jacob's days were sometimes hard to fill. This situation pleased Esau who hurried from this job to the next, eager to do all he was asked to do, and with the idea that he alone was doing all the work and more, even Jacob's share, while Jacob stayed in the carriage shed.

Then Doctor Fletcher took quite an interest in Jacob, and it was as big a surprise to Esau as it was to the rest of the town when the doctor took Jacob on as a helper around the house – seven-thirty to six, lunch, Sundays off, a little money every two weeks. The work was not hard and it was the kind of security that Jacob felt when he first walked under the shading branches of the old oak trees. Besides, the doctor said Jacob could read the books in his library if he liked. The thought of Jacob sitting around reading books made Esau work all the harder. He even stocked barley out in the township until blisters came up between his thumb and pointing finger and got too raw and painful to let him continue.

Esau was silent and exhausted each night from his work. Jacob saw that Esau expected him to get all the meals and to keep the shed in order. As the days went by, Jacob learned as well that Esau was not interested in whatever Jacob might have been reading. Their nights were spent silently and separately; the one feeling his muscles prepare for tomorrow's work; the other thinking about what he had read in the Doctor's office that day.

So for the first time the twins were separated. The summer went by quickly.

Washing down the Crystal Palace for the County Fair one day that fall, Esau felt the air cooling and he worried about the carriage shed. He and Jacob had fixed it up some but Esau was afraid now that someone might think the shed was no place to live in winter, and that he and Jacob would be made to get out and find a warmer place. But, he said to himself, it wouldn't matter to Jacob. That doctor would take care of him.

When he finished mopping the floor and had replaced the trestle tables around the walls, the caretaker came in and said, "Now, I think we're all set. The ladies'll like that clean floor. You come down to the gate for your money now, then run along home. How about that?"

Home. Esau stood on the road outside the gates to the Fair Grounds and looked towards the town. The oak trees massed together were like a big umbrella without a handle, set down over the houses. The roof of leaves and branches was better than shingles and rafters. He was aware of the little noises of the town that were stopping for the night: the wind in the branches, the humpahumpa of the grist mill, the clank-kunk of the forge. New sounds came on for the evening: the sharp bang of a screen door, the crooning of chickens planning to roost, the muffled tolling of the Anglican bell for evensong. All the sounds of the town, spirit things without bodies, had clean-cut edges to them. That was the difference between him and Jacob, he decided.

peace / Small town peace (margin note)

Home. He looked back to the gates of the Fair Grounds. Whitewashed field stones cemented into four square pillars with cement balls on top, spider-web-looking iron gates between each pillar and dinky sentry-boxes where they sold tickets. For Esau they stood for the silver dollar the caretaker had just given him in exchange for all the dreary work he'd done. And Esau knew that for Jacob the field-stone pillars would stand for bright sunshine, laughing around the grand stand, too many soda pops, and the rough city voices of car-nival men at night.

He started into town running, and the feel of running,

running anywhere, was good. Under the oaks it was cooler and he put his hands in his pockets and jogged along past the freight sheds, past the chick hatchery, by the jewellers, by the shoe repair and gents' furnishings, then trotted up the lane behind the Queen's Hotel.

This was home. How about that, mister caretaker?

He saw that Jacob was starting the fire when he came in. He bolted the double doors behind him, then crawled up in the straw loft to close the ventilator holes. Jacob was still busy with the fire and the frying-pan when he came down. Esau sat down in the old wing chair by the window that looked out on a tangle of weeds and rusting iron junk. Jacob couldn't see him here and Esau cried.

There was a hard sudden frost that night and Jacob and Esau cuddled together for warmth in the straw. In the morning there was snow drifted under the doors. Jacob woke up and looked at the snow powdered on the floor. He nudged Esau. Esau didn't wake up. He nudged again and said "Esau, look, it snowed last night." There was no answer. He toppled Esau over on his back. Esau was having a spell.

Jacob got dressed and ran out. He was back in a few minutes with Doctor Fletcher. Jacob was excited. The doctor was calm. He worked on Esau for a little while and the boy came around.

"This is no place for a boy in your condition," the doctor said. "We'll have to get you out of here."

Esau's eyes closed to slits and tears squeezed out. "No, no, you mustn't take us out of here," he cried. "We're all right. We've got to stay here."

The doctor left and Esau lay pale and still, blinking up at the shed rafters, not sorting the sounds of the town the way he liked to. Jacob was uncomfortable and shy because of the spell, and not able to do anything for Esau. At last he cleared his throat and looked down at the still figure in the straw.

"Wonder why they don't let Gerry play down the lane or around the shed here."

Esau sat up straight in the straw. It was no effort for him. He leaned close to Jacob.

"Because the Kennedys think their kid is better than us. It's not that there's somebody in the carriage shed. It's because you and me are here. That's the way things are. We're Institute kids and he's not. They think that's better. That's the way things are. What are you going to do about it?"

Jacob found young Gerry Kennedy sweeping the unexpected snow off the side porch of the Queen's.

"Did your old lady ever tell you me and Esau are orphans?"

"I don't know. I guess so."

"Well, you're nothing but a punk kid. That's all." Jacob clenched his fists and the east wall of the hotel was as cold and silent as bricks in a picture. The sky was cold and blue. Gerry didn't do anything.

The sun burst out then and you could almost see the snow start to melt under it. Jacob traced his steps back to the carriage shed. Inside, Esau was sleeping. Jacob left the doors open to let the warmth of the sun come in. The snow outside was melting fast. Steam rose from the tarred roofs. It would be a clear, crisp night. It would be the first night of the County Fair and carnival.

When Esau woke up hungry, it was growing dark and the twins talked about the carnival for a while as Jacob got the meal ready.

"Guess I'll go," Jacob said.

"You'll need some money," Esau said.

"No. I got my ticket and fifty cents. That should be enough."

"Take two bits out of my pants anyway."

On his way to the carnival, Jacob looked back at the shed slumped in the weeds, Esau inside and weak from a spell.

Ahead there was a strange glow of yellow over Geddes's store. He walked down the street beside Geddes's and across the bridge. He shrugged his shoulders up in his pea jacket and pressed outward with his ribs. His copper-toed boots clanked on the iron bridge for twelve steps, then he was in the trampled grass field of the carnival. Here were the growling city voices, the pure colours and lights with the night around blacker than he'd ever imagined.

He walked from tent to tent, looking at the prizes, listening to the barkers, looking at their faces, wondering what he would answer if one were to speak directly to him. He passed along the row of tents, inspected the merry-go-round and Ferris wheel at the far end, then came back along the other row of tents to the roped-off entrance. When he got there he had a clear picture of the carnival in his mind. There were no hidden parts of it. No unknown corners. It wasn't much. He was proud of himself because the carnival couldn't swallow him up in its noise and lights. He thought of Esau having a spell. He wondered what started a spell. Esau seemed frightened when the doctor brought him around. Frightened of what? Darn all spells anyway.

He rubbed his fifty-cent piece against the quarter Esau had given him. That's funny. Esau has a spell, wakes up frightened, doesn't want to leave the shed, makes him take two bits for the carnival. That's funny.

Alison arrived then with her father and brother. Jacob found the courage to speak and smile to her. Her father noticed him and waved his walking-stick in a greeting. She smiled quickly at him as they passed.

He watched her father buy tickets for the fun house. Alison followed her brother in. Jacob followed them. There was a labyrinth of mirrors first and Jacob heard Alison laughing on ahead. Then there was the winding tunnel of terror. Allie held back, nervous, laughing. She came to a turn where a stuffed owl blinked at her from a dimly lighted perch.

Kinda creepy.

"Allie, is that you, Allie?"

"Oh gracious. Who's that?"

"It's me, Jacob. That's all."

"You shouldn't sneak up behind me like that."

"I'm sorry. Wait Allie, wait. Allie?"

"What is it you want?"

"May I come up to your place tomorrow for a little while?"

"I don't know. You'll have to ask Daddy." She was gone past the owl light. He heard her footsteps in the tunnel.

"Be careful, Allie," he called. He stumbled back through the maze of mirrors out to her father.

"Sir, could I please call on Allie for a little while tomorrow afternoon?"

"Sure, Jacob, come on over tomorrow. Maybe Allie will serve something nice to eat in the drawing-room. That be all right?"

Jacob walked out of the blaze of yellow and noise. He reached the road and ran. The quick clank-clank of his own feet on the iron bridge drummed out all sounds of the carnival. This was something like it. He hurried around Geddes's corner, past Weaver's barber shop, around the Queen's Hotel and up the lane to the shed, eager to talk to Esau.

Esau was sitting up in the old wing chair. "Carnival over already?"

"I didn't stay. Here's your two bits. I didn't need it."

"Didn't you like it? What'd you do?"

"I found out how I can fix that punk kid, that's what I did. I know now. I got it all figured out."

Esau nodded his head and noticed Jacob was restless. Esau walked carefully from the chair to the pile of straw. He curled up under the patchwork quilts and waited.

They cuddled together. They made the straw warm under them. They heard the people walking home from the carnival. They wondered whether they heard Alison's footsteps.

During the night while Esau was asleep, Jacob whispered, "Don't let me do it. I don't want to do it. I know how, but it doesn't have anything to do with her."

The next morning Jacob knew something had happened at the carnival that was bad and wrong. He set the fire for breakfast. Esau watched him. Jacob said, "I ain't going to do anything about it."

"About what?"

"What happened last night." Jacob's back was to Esau as he got the cedar sticks blazing in the rusty stove. He turned and stood over Esau. Esau was pale. His finger-nails showed blue against the grey quilt. His mouth was open a little. His eyelids quivered.

"You going to have another spell?"

"No."

"There's the water and stuff. I left the draught on. I got to go to the Doc's now."

In the cool morning Jacob remembered the carnival and was ashamed.

The doctor asked how Esau was. Jacob said he was pale and weak and that his finger-nails were a funny colour.

"Well now, don't worry boy. I've got to go down to the hotel to see Mrs. Kennedy. I'll pop in on Esau while I'm there."

"Gerry's maw sick?"

"Yes, pretty sick."

The doctor left. He walked up the street and reached the lane back of the hotel. He looked down the lane, then up at the hotel. He turned in the lane to the shed where Esau lay.

The boy had had another spell. His face was pinched and he was unconscious. The doctor stayed in the shed for longer than he had planned. He worked carefully and got Esau breathing regularly and easily.

"You can't take many more of those, boy. Why don't you lay off?"

That night when he came back to the shed, Jacob said, "Missis Kennedy died this morning."

"Yeah?"

"Yeah and Mister Kennedy's sore as a boil, they say, on account of the doctor wouldn't go and see her when he said he would."

"When's the funeral?"

"Day after tomorrow, I guess."

"You better go."

"To a funeral? What for?"

"The Kennedys let us stay in the shed for nothing. You go to the funeral and that's a way of thanking Mister Kennedy."

"Why don't you go?"

"I was sick again this morning."

"Another spell?"

"Guess so. The Doc was here when I came to and I was weak as a kitten. Still am."

"Look, I can't go to a funeral. I never saw a stiff."

"You don't have to look at her."

"I got no clothes."

"You'll look all right. Wear my copper-toed boots. They're in better shape than yours."

"I don't want to go."

"You'll go. It won't be bad."

"But it's a funeral, Esau. I'm scared."

"Look, Mister Kennedy is doing us a favour. One of us has got to go. That's all."

Jacob went. He scrubbed his face and hands, brushed his clothes and wore Esau's boots.

The big oaks looked old and wintry as he walked under them to the Anglican church. He thought of the June day when he and Esau walked the other way on these streets, and then the bell started tolling.

The church was full. The men and women were still. The organ and the bell were sad. Staring hard at Mr. Kennedy's back, Jacob didn't want to stay, but it wasn't Mr. Kennedy's fault and it wasn't the doctor's fault and it wasn't Esau's fault.

Gerry had gotten him into this too. His feet itched and he wanted to get closer to the mourners' bench where Gerry sat beside his father. Jacob moved quietly across the back of the church. Nobody noticed. He got to the other aisle. When the funeral man came in to open the top half of the coffin lid, everybody sat up to stare. Mrs. Palson grasped the wheels of her wheel-chair and moved a little closer. Jacob thought he'd make it to the empty end of the mourners' bench.

Somebody laid a firm hand on his shoulder and a quiet voice said, "Jacob, how are you, lad? Haven't seen you in a dog's age. Where's Esau?" It was big Audie Seaton. Jacob looked up at the plain face and he wondered where Esau was too.

Then the funeral began and it was too late. Jacob went home and sat by his tack trunk, not speaking. Esau waited. Finally, Jacob said, "I guess I came close to doing something pretty bad in church. I wanted to get at him but I was stopped."

Cuddling against his brother for warmth in the straw, Jacob wanted only to say he was sorry for what had happened at the carnival and at the funeral. He didn't know who to say it to.

So Esau died that night as suddenly as you say it. Jacob looked at the body in terror. He went out of the shed and the day was cold and clear. That helped to make him feel the truth of Esau's death.

"Yes, it must have been a considerable decision," Doctor Fletcher said, as though he were talking about something else. Jacob looked at him helplessly.

"You know, boy, you look a lot like your mother now."

"What are we going to do about a funeral and all that?" Jacob asked.

"We've got to give him back, don't we?"

"He was good to me, Doctor Fletcher."

"Oh I'm sure he was. They usually are, but this other thing, the spell and whatever it was he wanted you to do, that was what wore him out. Imagine. A boy of sixteen burned right out."

"He always wanted to know who our mother was. Or is. He used to think she was still around."

"She is, Jacob. You'll be able to find her now."

"Why didn't you tell us where she was before?"

"Because you're free now. The rest'll be easy."

Free? But Esau was good to me. We had a fine time together in the orphanage and in the carriage shed.

Jacob left the doctor's house, cold in the heart now, bewildered by what the doctor had said. The doctor talked to him as though his mind was on something else all the time. Jacob walked on towards the centre of town, towards the carriage shed. The oak leaves were turning to shrivelled black green. They had the dry rattle of fall and there was no warmth. The shed. He couldn't go there. Esau wasn't there. But where to go? Back to the doctor's or to the Aid? He didn't know what to do. He kept on.

In the shed, the unbleached cotton sheet on the straw still held Esau's shape. The undertaker had taken the body hours ago.

Jacob packed his things in the tack trunk, carried it out to the street and looked back at the shed for the last time.

Then big Audie Seaton came along the street and stood beside Jacob for a while. Jacob finally turned to him and said, "I'm glad you stopped to talk to me in the church the other day. It was good."

"Boy, I always like to stop and talk. You remember that."

Then Gerry Kennedy came out of the side door of the Queen's and put one foot up on Jacob's trunk. "I hope you don't mean to be mad at me, Jacob."

"No, I'm not mad at anybody. I want to be friends."

Then Alison came along. She was in a buggy driven by her father. They did a U-turn on the wide cold street. Alison's father looked down on Jacob and said, "There, boy. It's bad but try not to take it too hard."

Alison stood beside Jacob, watching him as her father spoke. Jacob turned to her.

She whispered: "When it's all over, come to our house for a visit. You asked to, remember?"

"I won't be able to come, Allie, thank you very kindly." Jacob looked from her to Gerry. Allie frowned and hurried back to the buggy. Her father clucked at the horse and they went out of sight around the corner of the Queen's Hotel.

Then Doctor Fletcher came driving down the street from the other direction in his buggy. He stepped down and hoisted Jacob's trunk into the back. He put a hand on Jacob's elbow and led him to the buggy. Jacob got in wearily. The doctor got in beside him and they drove away.

THREE

The listeners

YOUNG AUDIE SEATON was seven when his mother made him blow the egg.

She admitted to herself later that she had put it off too long in his case and should never have gone through with it. But she had timed it just right with Audie's two little brothers and she was bound she wouldn't leave Audie out of it.

Audie really remembered blowing the egg when he grew up. His mother would certainly never have told him about blowing the egg. (It wasn't like the time he sat in a pail of milk in the barn one night, thinking it was a milking stool. She told him about that over and over again. That was one of her memories.) Blowing the egg was a pure memory all his own. It always bothered him.

A man doesn't keep too many pure memories of when he was practically a baby. The nice memories all run together into a kind of pleasant feeling you can't describe. The bad ones, the unexplained ones, they sort of keep hidden and pop up to the surface like marsh gas, but only once in a long while.

The last time Audie told about himself blowing the egg, he remembered being troubled for his father while he was doing it. His father is big Audie Seaton, the old man who still drives to church in a horse and buggy. Young Audie remembered his mother kept asking him if he heard what she was saying about his father. Audie remembered crying, gasping for air and hiccuping in limp despair. He remembered trying to blow out the egg and watching the last drip of yellow fall off the egg into a blue striped bowl. His mother took the blown egg from him, sealed the pin holes with jar wax, and put it in the box on the top shelf of the sideboard in the best room. That was young Audie's memory of it.

The day his wife finally died, big Audie set to work with the fence stretchers, hammer and staples, straightening up the fence along the front of the farm. Somebody would drive up in a rig, big Audie would listen to them, then say, "Now that's good of you to come and say that to me. Do you want to go in and see her? She's in the best room. Walk right in." Then he'd get back to the fence.

Young Audie did the chores as usual, the day she died, but the first chance he got, when he was sure big Audie was out mending his fence, he went in behind the coffin, stood on a chair to reach the top shelf of the sideboard, and brought down the box.

There were three blown eggs in it, sealed with yellowy-old wax at both ends, dried and lightened by the years. One was Audie's. The other two, he decided, were blown by his brothers. He left the box on the kitchen table.

The brothers came home for the funeral. One brother arrived in a new car and left it parked with the doors wide open under the leaning pear tree by the front door. The pallbearers bumped their arms against the car when they brought the coffin out on the day of the funeral. The other brother came by train and rode out from the station to the farm in the express wagon. Beside young Audie they stood, white and city-looking, as though the light would go right through them.

As soon as they came in the kitchen, young Audie said, "Look what I found up in the sideboard." The brothers looked at the old eggs and waited for Audie to say something about them. Audie never said anything. He waited for them to say something. They went out the back door, down to the barn to look around.

When the funeral was all over, with his mother buried easy out beyond the Fair Grounds, with his father still busy at the fence out front, and his brothers back in the city, Audie discovered quiet for the first time. The house was like the skating rink in summer, empty, and outside noises bouncing around to make it quieter.

It came on Audie all of a sudden that he had nobody. Nothing was left but this house with all its friendly places, the slidy old sofa that was a cool place for reading on Sundays, the hired man's room where there was an oval picture of two white horses with their thin noses distended, the cistern in the cellar where his mother kept the butter to cool, where he used to keep his home-made root beer, where his aunt used to go last summer to sneak her cigarettes so big Audie wouldn't know.

All this and the memory no one could explain. No one. Big Audie? Too busy fixing his fence, tipping his straw hat so politely, watching the cars go down the road and around the corner. His brothers? Strangers that didn't speak up and the sun could shine through. A bare, hurting memory.

It must have started when Audie's mother was in high school. For school, she always wore a starched middy and tunic with her hair loose and nice down the back. She tossed her hair a lot because she talked with spirit and wondered and asked questions and told how she felt about things the other girls never thought much about. She was never still.

Walking down the hill from the school to home one day, she told her girl friends that this old town, with all its oak trees shrouding down and the people in it, was the world. The whole world. If the land goes on in all directions from this town, she said, and there are more towns, bigger and smaller, it doesn't make any difference because the whole world is in this town.

There are people waiting in this town, she said. Waiting to die, waiting to be loved, waiting to love, waiting for the loneliness. And there are people who have given up in this town, she said. Given up loving, given up hope, given up promising, given up living in order to die.

It sounded wrong because it didn't seem cheerful to her girl friends, and they put it away in their minds to watch her later on to see how she'd turn out.

Young Audie's mother is still talked about by the old men at the train station. There was an afternoon when she was in high school when she was at the station watching and listening. The telegraph lines sang in the wind and she wanted to hear the voices, and it was a singing hum so she walked over to the tracks, satisfied. There were no voices. Only under the oaks were there voices. She put one foot on a track and waited. Soon there was the whistle from around the bend, then the track quivered a little. The train shuffaclanked in and stopped. Some people got off the train and walked over to the covered democrat that would take them down the road. She asked the driver where he was going. He looked down at her and said, "Nowhere."

See? You're not going anywhere, she said to herself. You'll be driven out and off the end and never come back.

The day telegraph operator came out to stretch his legs. She got in step with him and walked up and down the platform with him.

"You waste a lot of time," she said, "sitting in there taking all that stuff down, bringing it all in when it's all here already. There's no need for any more. What did you do today? You took down a hurting telegram from an angry man in the city to an angry man in town. You took down a lonely telegram from outside to a lonely woman in town. You took down some lies about business from a liar in the city to a liar in town. You took down a sympathetic telegram from a man in the city afraid to come out to the funeral of his dead friend. Why don't you just put it all into the back of that democrat over there? The driver says he isn't going anywhere. You'd be doing the town some good."

That was the kind of girl she was. Her girl friends told each other it was all stuff, but they'd keep an eye on her anyway.

But that was the kind of life she vowed she'd lead when she got married. She was sure she'd marry right, and have good children, and she'd pass on her driven way of the world to them and they'd turn out all right. Not just lumps, she said.

So it was a real big surprise when the news got around that she was going to marry big Audie Seaton.

Imagine. Big Audie Seaton. Kind of a handy man around town. You could get Audie to do almost any kind of odd job you needed done. The only regular jobs he had were the high school lawn and garden during spring and summer, and keeping the L.O.L. hall heated and swept out in winter.

Big Audie lived on the town line just back of the high school. He came to town when he was a boy about seventeen. Somebody bought a patch of six acres from the Framinghams and gave it to big Audie. That first year was a funny one. He wasn't exactly a farmer, so he couldn't come in and stand around talking Saturday nights with the others, and he wasn't exactly a town man, so he couldn't get along so well with the regulars in Weaver's barber shop during the week.

He was big, friendly, easy-going. When he fell in love with young Audie's mother he let her know he was bound to spruce up and make a real home for her.

A young bride walking around her house the summer of her wedding day: warty old toads, toads in the hot bed on the south side of the house where the sun made the tomato plants grow; a humming-bird pulling back on the invisible threads of food in each flower of a delphinium spike; a rabbit in the patch of English violets; a coon up the basswood tree at the gate; heifers and steers gadded by the heel fly down along the fence and back. All is living. All is living but dear Auden. What letters he wrote before. Loving letters, but now never living when we come together, and this the summer of our wedding day.

"I guess I just ain't much on chickens," he said instead. "Beef cattle's what we should be into. But you get a few chickens anyway. Keep them in the woodshed."

There was a bad, dry spring the year after they were married. Big Audie put four acres of river-bottom land into potatoes, but the ground went street hard. A couple plants got through. It was failure. Big Audie was bowed by it and never once looked down to the river bottom that summer.

Cleaning up and fussing around in the woodshed, the way women do, young Audie's mother said, "I mustn't bother dear Audie now, the way he's so worried over the potatoes. Pretty nearly a year now. The time is long gone and past. Speaking from the heart isn't hard. He can do it. We can. He'll get over the potatoes. He'll be feeling better. I'll wait."

The hens in their orange-crate nests stirred and clucked a little. She closed the woodshed door. She had a feeling in her like a cut finger touching the vinegar jug.

Other than the potatoes, that first year was a good one. A baby boy, young Audie, was born. She remembered. Not just a lump. No, not just a lump.

Big Audie, he fairly purred. Some people asked would he purr for long, but most said big Audie was a family man. And this was good, the baby boy.

A year went by. The owner of the grist mill wouldn't give big Audie credit on five tons of lime until the potato crop was off. Big Audie wanted the lime for a piece of pasture he'd rented from the Framinghams. So he had to nail up all the old barrels he could lay hands on and ship out the potatoes.

So big Audie was in the drive-shed, whaling away at the barrels, working late into the nights. In the woodshed one night, after the supper dishes were done and young Audie asleep, his mother sat on an up-ended sugar bag in front of the nests.

This is what the hens heard: "That man's working too hard. He wants that lime so bad. Working all night. Coming to bed beat. Not saying anything. Not looking at the baby. Just beat and worried. He'll get his lime though. Married a year and a half. A son. Still it hasn't happened. Maybe once he knew what a marriage was and what a family was, but he can't seem to remember now for lime, potatoes and work. And I can't worry him now. I'll have to wait until things are better. Time's passing. But I'm young. It hurt bad last year before the baby. Then it got all right for a while. It's bad again but I don't feel it so much, somehow."

She got up slowly, waved her hand towards the hens in the nests, then turned around and unlocked herself out of the woodshed and into the back kitchen.

Fixing for bed that night, she got to remembering what it used to be like walking home from school, watching and listening around the train station. Sure, they were lumps all right, but it was exciting.

The third year did it. There was another baby. Big Audie spent six weeks in bed with a fever. There was a mortgage arranged on the house so he could pay three years' rent on a pasture farm that was empty across from the Framinghams.

Young Audie's mother never heard about the mortgage directly. She just knew she'd lost big Audie for good. When he got over the fever, he told her a little about the mortgage and she started to say something; but he went out the back door to the barn, hitched up the team and drove out the lane. She could hardly wait for him to get off the place by then, but he was patient and slow with the team, cinching up the belly-bands and tugs carefully, taking the twists out of the lines. He went finally. He took a load of barley and oats to be ground at the mill. As soon as she heard the rattle of the bridge boards

under his wagon wheels, <u>she locked herself in the woodshed.</u>
The hens shuffled uneasily in their straw.

This is what they heard: "That man. Haven't ever known
him. It isn't fair. Goodness knows I opened up to him right
from the start. I was never shy. Goodness knows living is not
all up to me. But no, more pasture, more steers, more lime. A
mortgage. Three years I've kept putting it off. Something had
better happen soon. He wanted me for more than, well, you
know, when we got married. Now he acts like he doesn't need
me. If it doesn't happen soon."

After two babies a woman's body shows what's in her heart
sometimes. She turned and the turning was tired. She
unlocked the woodshed and walked into the kitchen and the
walking was weary. Her third child was stirring in her by then
and she knew it would be the last.

He was born on their fourth wedding anniversary and big
Audie took more interest in this third baby than he did in
the first two. He gave Doctor Fletcher a box of cigars. Everything was going big Audie's way that year. A hundred acres
clear and free. Another hundred with a mortgage, the farm
where Johnson Mender used to live. Good white-face stock
and his one pure-bred bull. He hung around the main street
of town Saturday nights and <u>people took to calling him
Mister Seaton.</u> They'd had to get somebody else to look after
the L.O.L. hall and the high school grounds long before this.
People'd pretty well forgotten about big Audie doing the
like of that.

And it was all settled in young Audie's mother's mind. The
years went by. Big Audie kept on shipping a few more head
each fall. There was a lot of talk about him for reeve, but it
never came to anything. He bought a car for their seventh
wedding anniversary, but young Audie's mother didn't think
much about it.

It was a drizzle day in October. Big Audie was shipping.
Three truck-loads, he figured when he left in the morning.

The boys were playing together in the orchard. Young Audie's mother had redded up the breakfast dishes and was ready to read the paper the way she always did. Instead, she went out into the woodshed. She stroked the neck feathers of the laying hens. The hens dipped their heads nervously as her hand moved, gently, nervously.

This is what the hens heard: "I'm through. It's come to this. I've got to tell someone. Someone. I've got to warn the boys somehow, but still don't want to hurt their father."

She felt under each hen. They lifted their wings warily and gave low, growling cluck noises.

"Hurry, hurry," she whispered.

She waited in the kitchen, watching the orchard and listening for noises from the woodshed. Finally there came a burst of cackle. She called young Audie in, then hurried to the woodshed. She took the warm egg from under the hen. In the kitchen she told young Audie everything. Her voice was mill-pond calm. She told him everything from the time she was in high school to that day. Young Audie smiled a little while she talked and paid close attention when she talked about Daddy. Then she told him to blow the egg out. He did it nervously. It was done quickly. She sealed the egg with wax and put it in a box.

There was another cackle from the woodshed. She called the second boy in and got another warm egg. Again it was done. She had to blow most of the egg because the boy giggled when he set to blowing. Then it was the youngest boy's turn. He stared at the blue bowl as she talked. He cried and his face went red as he tried to blow the egg. His mother blew most of this egg too, but the boy calmed enough to blow the last yellow drops into the bowl. She smiled at him and patted him out the door. Young Audie was waiting and he put his arm around the shoulders of the youngest boy for a moment.

It was all over. Done, done, done. She went into the best room, closed the doors, and sat at one end of the slidy sofa.

Come in to me now, dear Auden, big Audie, Mister Seaton, father of such fine boys. Three of them. Imagine. Beef prices good this fall, Mister Seaton? Oh, do sit down and talk to me. You what? You have something to say? Then do speak to your dear wife.

I know we haven't been very close the last few years and it's been hard going. It took a long time to sink in, but as I was loading cattle today I saw the muck on my boots and had an awful fear that you weren't real, that it was a dream of mine that I had a family waiting for me. Then I was afraid bad, and had to know did they wait for me, or want me or what. And I came. You've worked hard and never once complained.

Oh stop, Audie. What's wrong?

Her tears were sad, not violent. No, it's too late and not close enough. You're trying but it's not close enough to the living. The hens know. The boys know, but they won't ever let on. I made sure of that. It's too late. It's all over.

There was no joy, no hint, even, of the old driven way of the world of hers. From where she sat on the sofa in the best room, she looked up suddenly at the locked double doors that connected with the dining-room and said, "Once there was a time, dear Auden, but it's all gone out of me. All out of me. I guess all I can do is go on this way."

FOUR

You'll get the rest of him soon

Doctor Fletcher never let you forget that he was born in the house he lived in, that he left it only to go to medical school, that the table he used as a desk was the one where his mother had the final labour pains caused by him coming into this world. This pride of origin and unchange was hard to understand because the Fletcher house was an ordinary one on the ordinary street beside the Fair Grounds. Nothing distinguished it except perhaps the brick wall across the front of the lot put up by the doctor the year he graduated. Behind the house, the tangled garden grew right up to the back of the grand stand of the Fair Grounds. Only a wire fence separated the doctor's garden from the toilets under the grand stand. It wasn't as bad as it sounds. The Fair Grounds were used only four days in the year: Dominion Day for the harness horse races and three days in September for County Fair. Besides, the Fair Board always got someone to douse the galvanized troughs with disinfectant, so it was a sanitary smell.

One Dominion Day, Froody had to go to the bathroom three times. Lemonade from the W.I. booth, two bottles of soda pop, the fun of telling everybody about her baby brother born a few days earlier, it was no wonder.

(Aunt Cress claims there has always been something queer about the family kidneys ever since Froody's grandfather got kicked there by a string-halted brood mare. Nobody believes this any more.)

On her third visit, the sun and the powerful smell of disinfectant made Froody feel dizzy suddenly. She ran in behind the women's toilet, close beside Fletcher's fence. She was sure she was going to be terribly sick.

She didn't remember much. Doctor Fletcher was scrouched down in the long weeds in the back end of his yard, near where Froody was leaning on the fence. He had a trowel in one hand and a pad of cotton batting in the other. He scooped out a shallow hole in the grass. He shook something tiny and pink off the cotton pad into the hole, then replaced the sod, tamping it back in place neatly with both hands. Then he mumbled for maybe as much as a minute. All Froody heard clearly was "you'll get the rest of him soon."

"You'll get the rest of him soon," Froody heard, mumbled by a friend of the family, a nice old man, the doctor. This was the man who was there when mother got the baby at the hospital eight days ago. Froody couldn't patch it together: the words, what the doctor was doing, the adult knowledge all doctors must have, her knowing this wasn't right for the doctor and that she was not supposed to see or hear.

Froody went home from the Fair Grounds to lie down and be delicate for a while, the way Aunt Cress does now when she pulls the blinds down in the best room and half lies, half sits with a wet towel on her forehead. Not sick exactly, but just leave me alone and quiet. I'll be all right in the morning.

Out of the sun, away from the crowd, Froody lay in her own room, listening to the baby squalling minutely for his four-o'clock feeding. Leaf shadows wavered on the floor by the bed. The trees in the yard, big old oaks, nodded and turned their branches in the wind. The sun was on its way down beyond the Fair Grounds. Froody forgot her sickness.

In the darkening room she remembered one time when Doctor Fletcher told her mother boys were a sight better than girls. "Boys stand a better chance," he had said, "especially the ones I look after." That happened a long time ago when Froody had gyppy tummy. Her mother went red in the face, she remembered, and shooed the doctor out of the room. It was the one particular memory of Doctor Fletcher that Froody had. She fell asleep trying to fit it with what she had seen at the Fair Grounds that afternoon.

She woke up hungry and Dominion Day a great disappointment to her. She wished she had heard all the speeches.

County Fair time came around and it rained to beat skin hell all three days of it, so the races, the outdoor exhibits and the midway were called off. They couldn't call off the ploughing match, though, because the winners had to go on to the big Inter-County plough-off first week of October.

The ploughing events went on in the rain. At nights the men in the tractor classes backed their machines under the grand stand out of the rain so they'd start easily the following morning.

One night, Honey Salkald – he was in love with Froody that year – backed his John Deere under the grand stand, turned it off and climbed down. He stretched his legs a little and wiggled at his ears with his fingers to try and stop the humming that was still there.

He was soaked right through to the skin, but he stood out in the rain and let it soak in some more. It didn't matter. Walking up and down to get the stiffness out of his knees, he was close to Doctor Fletcher's back fence. First Honey heard the clink of metal. Then he saw a flashlight beam in the long grass. Honey walked over to ask who it was.

The sky was a deep grey, nearly black, but grey enough to show a man's silhouette. There the doctor was, standing up straight with his arms up above his head, looking down into the grass.

The doctor sounded a lot like an Anglican minister, Honey said later. *pass gossip on...*

"Seventy years isn't much, the way you keep track of it," the doctor said, "a breathing spell while you wait for the rest of him. You'll feel him growing from now on; a little restless in a few years; then an urgent longing; then the discoveries and finally the contentment. Nourish him the way you do all of us. Be patient with him because you'll get the rest of him soon. There is no question of reward."

Of course, Honey couldn't remember anything that long, but that's what the doctor was saying. Naturally, with Honey one of the regulars at Weaver's barber shop, it soon got all over town that old Doc Fletcher was going queer.

It was like any story that spreads. Froody heard about it, so she told Annie Somebody-or-other what happened Dominion Day. Annie told her father who worked for Mr. Steever. Mrs. Steever whispered it to Froody's mother at the next meeting of the W.I. So Froody's story came back to her and, in a manner of speaking, the grade-A-large stamp was on the fact. Poor old Doctor Fletcher was queer.

How it was was described as gospel truth, even by people who had not heard Froody's or Honey's eye-witness accounts directly. Eventually these accounts came back to Froody and Honey, but without their names connected. So it was true. Poor old Doctor Fletcher was queer.

The nurses at the hospital laughed. Sure, Doc was queer. The poor old man had been delivering babies since the year the railroad came through: delivering babies and watching people die and wishing the breathing ones would leave him alone.

That was the thing about Doctor Fletcher. He kept to himself. He played a lone hand. He got along fine with his housekeeper and with everybody at the hospital. After hours he was sometimes a hard man to deal with. He didn't want work ever to interfere. He had things on his mind and things didn't include the people of the town or what they did.

He explained it as best he could. He said, sure, he was old Doctor Fletcher, but there was the somebody who wasn't the doctor. I got a life of my own outside of babying and operating, he said, and that life's got to be lived else I'm nobody. Like Weaver, he said. He barbers and gossips and that's all. What's wrong is there's too many hair-cutting gossips, he said. They're just people, snicking away at it all the time.

Another thing, he said, they always try to make people out of the ones that don't want to be. See, there's a big difference between being somebody and being people. And when you know they're out to snick you, the doctor said, you got to beat them the hell off.

But the permanent standing committee on membership at the Lodge wouldn't leave the doctor alone. They wanted him initiated.

"Doctor Fletcher belongs in the Lodge," they always said. "It don't seem right, somehow, that he ain't a member," they always said. Doctor Fletcher refused to join.

"I'm not a joiner, boys," he said. "Besides, I don't like scalloped potatoes and chicken croquettes much." Lodge met Thursdays in the Queen's Hotel for lunch. Usually that was what was on the menu. The doctor always said "no" in a nice way, like that.

Later on in the fall, long after County Fair, when there was nothing much doing around town, the permanent standing committee went at the doctor again. The three of them, Muncey, Weaver and Sobel, walked over to the Fletcher place, knocked on the front door and got no answer. They looked at each other without saying anything, then walked around to the back yard. You see, this was a kind of show-down visit. After the stories that were going around, the Lodge wasn't sure the old doctor was the right sort to be in. But they'd give him one more chance. That was what was in Muncey, Weaver and Sobel: one more chance for old Doc Fletcher and a chance for him to explain away the queer stories going around about him, if he could.

Sure enough, he was down in the cold, wet grass by the back fence. The membership committee sort of broke apart. They looked smaller than when they were walking together. They heard the doctor mumbling. Muncey said Honey hit it just right: old Doc did sound like an Anglican minister.

Sobel coughed and the doctor looked around. He motioned them to go away, then hunched his shoulders as though to crowd them back from his distance.

"Doc, we came to ask you about joining the Lodge again. We want to talk serious this time. You been putting us off up to now." Weaver's voice was part bantering, part whining.

"Get out of my yard," the doctor said, then turned, stood up and faced the three men. "Get out. This is my private yard where I want to be left alone. Get out." He walked toward them, swinging the trowel in his hand a little.

They got out all right, but Weaver was mad. Weaver told the young staff doctor at the hospital what had happened. This doctor was a Lodge brother, or whatever you call it. He'd joined another branch of it in the city when he was interning, so, the way they figured it, he, Muncey, Weaver and Sobel were brothers.

It was talked around considerable and Doctor Fletcher was finally brought up on the carpet. Then he got the letter from the Hospital Board. That was the day it all came to an end.

He read the letter after breakfast. Then he walked down to the barber shop with the letter in one hand. He stood in front of Weaver, close to him to make him stop his work, and said, "You did this to me because I wouldn't join your Lodge. You got to butter yourself up by imagining a man would want to belong to it. Well, you're wrong, mister, dead wrong. I'll rot in a box before you initiate me."

That did it. Weaver put down his clippers and grabbed the receiver off the wall phone. "That you, Muncey?" he said. "The Doc's got his letter from the Hospital Board."

From far away, and metallic, Muncey's voice was a clatter out of the receiver. What he said made Weaver lift his shoulders and screw up his face in embarrassment. He put his hand over the mouthpiece to prevent himself from making another mistake. He stared around him at the men in his shop. He hung up. Honey Salkald got up, staring back at Weaver. The others got up too and waited for Honey to speak.

"You better take my name off that list, too, Weaver," Honey said. Then he went out the door left open by Doctor Fletcher.

The doctor left Weaver's barber shop and went directly to the hospital. He figured it was about time to fix up Mrs. Scorrel's baby boy and send them both home. In the reception hall of the hospital (Doctor Fletcher saw nothing but the baked apron and the neatly pressed white duck trousers) the young doctor told him that all arrangements had been made for Mrs. Scorrel and that he, the young doctor, would be glad to look after post-natal.

Doctor Fletcher went into the maternity room and saw Mrs. Scorrel and the eight-day-old baby boy. For the moment everything was real and there in the bassinet was <u>another chance, another novice, another initiate. He smiled at the word and the baby.</u> *? ? ? What?*

But when he walked by the superintendent's office, there was the girl waiting in the doorway for him. With the pay envelope. He understood then, at last.

His housekeeper found him that night about dusk. He was face down in the wet grass at the back of the yard. She put her arms up and out to show how he was. When they picked him up to carry him into the house, his mark was left in the fluffy snow that had fallen. Froody burst into terrible tears for a girl her age.

FIVE

A room, a light for love

S HE WAS ALONE in the hotel apartment. Little familiar winter noises came through the windows. Her heart was full of expectation as she got up. Her mind was content with the new peace and order of the hotel.

Bent over the marble wash-bowl, washing her hair, she noticed the freshly cleaned rug on the floor. Bending her head a little more, she got a brief, awkward glimpse of the clean window and freshly painted woodwork.

Gerald won't expect this when he comes home, but if he's thought about the hotel at all, this is the way he wants it to be: practically full of guests, rooms cleaned and newly painted, the dining-room full – Saturdays and Sundays in particular.

A fresh start for Gerald, a fresh start – the way he wants it. She rinsed her hair a second time, then sat by the clinking old radiator, rubbing her hair dry with a towel. It was silky, coppery-red and long – almost misty as it came dry. She held a handful out from her head and looked, smiling. What would it be like not having red hair? What would it be like not to have been called "Carrot-top" in school? She drifted easily into the new, yet already familiar dream: how really different is a red-headed person from the others? How different can a red-headed person be? She fingered the long, curling ends idly. Longer than when Gerald saw it last. Not so orange-coloured. She reached into the dresser drawer for her tortoise-shell combs. Her hand touched the unfamiliar box and she changed her mind.

A fresh start for Gerald, so let's wear his silver combs. She took them from the box and slipped them carefully into her hair, patting the piled-up waves neatly.

The silver-backed combs were his Christmas present to her. The old hurt of him not being home for Christmas came back. She hoped again, consciously, moving her lips, that it wouldn't be long. This time she felt her lips moving because, this time, she knew it wouldn't be long, that it would be tonight, and the hurt went away. She touched the combs again and reminded herself that it was a fresh start for Gerald. She dressed slowly with a distinct new pleasure. As she put the thin gold watch into her starched blouse pocket, the town-hall clock bonged noon.

Catherine, one of the new girls, brought lunch to her on a tray. The girl, her face flushed a little from working in the steaming kitchen, was clumsy and embarrassed as she put the tray down. She tucked strands of loose, mousy hair back and wished hers would glisten like Alison's.

Then there was a loud rap at the open door and Jethro Geddes came in. He smiled to Alison, then nodded to Catherine who backed slowly and carefully to the door, trying to smile away her envy of Alison.

"Troop trains from the *Ascaria* get to the city tonight, Allie. I just heard over at the Armouries. Gerry may be on."

"Yes, I heard about the *Ascaria*. Oh, I do hope Gerald is on. Won't it be wonderful to have him back?"

They looked at each other in silence. Jeth's hands fluttered like white wings as he turned his black fur cap back and forth in front of him. His finely shaped head jutted cleanly out of the collar of his bulky mackinaw. Alison felt the strange old fear of Jeth she had felt before: the fear of a wanting man and the something else underneath, as though she liked the fear.

"Don't stare so, Jeth. You make me nervous."

"It's your hair, Allie. Beautiful."

"Oh go on, I just washed it." She was uncomfortable and lost for a moment. Then, she smiled widely and asked, "How's Lita?"

"Fine. She has a new dress to wear at Butlers' big party next week. Green thing with a big pleated skirt. Or maybe I shouldn't be talking about it."

"We'll be having a big party here. Sort of a home-coming party for Gerald." It came out of her in a strained, uncertain way, as though she didn't mean to say it just then.

"Party? Here? In the hotel?" Jeth smiled a waiting smile, the way you smile to encourage someone to tell the rest of a joke.

"Yes, here. I've had some work done in the old drawing-room on the second floor. It'll be there. You wait and see." She was defiant and proud.

"When Gerry comes home." Jeth pushed his jaw out so his teeth were clenched as he smiled. The jutting out of his head seemed to Alison more frightening than before, and there was more of that other feeling. She knew the mocking in his voice and she felt a sense of control – yes, that was it – control, knowing that he wanted her. She sat up straighter in her chair. He backed up to the door, still twirling his cap in his hands. He said good-bye and she listened to his running foot-steps all the way down to the main floor.

"When Gerry comes home," she said out loud, then stuck her tongue out at the empty doorway.

She sat at the secretary desk by the window and the thought of a fresh start for Gerald was strong in her. A fresh start for him and me. How different may a red-headed person be from the others?

The sun, low in the winter sky, had gotten around to the west and shone hard in the window. The yellowy-red light touched her bowed head.

She was crying tears of helpless waiting, tears of love for Gerry who wrote all the faithful letters that read to her the way he was when he left. They became tears of anger at Jeth for saying her hair was beautiful. She hoped it was, but it was for Gerald who was coming home at last.

She remembered the girl, Catherine, who backed awkwardly out of the room, then she thought of Jeth backing out of the room too, then of the meaning of Jeth, what was back of him. She stopped the tears proudly, felt the silver combs secure in her hair, and decided to go downstairs and look at the drawing-room. The new pride, the new confidence, they were strong in her too, and the love of Gerald was so delicate and beautiful she barely recognized it.

She walked down to the wide hallway on the second floor. The rich, new mulberry rug muffled her steps to the drawing-room. The high double doors clicked open into the room. The floor, newly cleaned and waxed, glistened warmly in the afternoon sun pouring through the three high windows. The grey wainscoting flashed long slivers of light as she moved across the floor. And the red wallpaper fairly shimmered in the light of day. It was a dazzling room, bright and alive, waiting, eager, Alison thought.

She walked along the wall with the windows in it. It was bare, but she saw gold-framed, gold-matted prints hanging between the windows; a row of chairs, all with needle-point seats, a sofa in here, maybe an aspidistra in a brass tub right there. She turned and looked at the opposite wall. There was no furniture there, but she saw arm-chairs in brown velvet, arranged in small groups. A parlour organ in the corner? Yes. She drew the heavy gold drapes across two of the windows and the room, rich, warm and comforting, glowed softly. A fresh start.

She drew the drapes across the third window, walked across the darkened floor, and opened the doors into the hall. The doors let a little light into the room. The light turned her eyes back for a last look. She could hardly leave, now that the decorating was finished. She looked up at the freshly painted ceiling. The thin strips of wood that latticed the ceiling were dark and gold and stood out against the pale cream plaster.

Alison decided the ceiling was best of all, except for a scar in the very middle. There had been a gas chandelier once, but Gerry's father had it taken down. Something would have to be done about that soon. She closed the doors at last, a little disappointed.

She went down to the lobby of the hotel. She looked around carefully. The young man sitting behind the clerk's desk got up as she came in and he touched the shock of hair over his forehead when she said good afternoon.

She smiled to him and thought again of Catherine and then Jeth, backing out of her room a few hours ago, and now this – like tugging at his forelock as milady drives by.

She hurried back upstairs. She knew at last what it was to be. She had discovered the pride in herself, the confidence, and the idea of control was new and compelling.

It was to be more than a new love for each other. She could feel a part of the answer to her new inquiring dream. The rich comforting feeling of the drawing-room was big enough for everybody. A ceiling like that would hold a lot of love. Things would be better now. Someone had said that to her not so long ago.

Later, the telegram came. A boy from the telegraph office told Alison to hurry right over. She sent him back to tell the operator the telegram could be delivered in the usual way.

So Gerald came home that night. The familiarity of the station and the night shapes of buildings he knew on both sides of the tracks were so exciting he wondered how he would control himself when he saw Allie for the first time in four years.

And, there she is! Oh God, Allie, God. Again the look of his wife in the wispy yellow light of the station was the dream he had kept all the time. It was what he expected to see, but seeing it at last was a bursting excitement in him.

They held each other for a moment there on the station platform.

"Happy new year, Allie," he whispered. His eyes filled with tears and he let them trickle down his cheeks. He'd wanted to cry ever since the ship docked.

They walked the two blocks to the hotel without speaking. They walked up the two flights of stairs without speaking. Gerry noticed changes inside the hotel and said nothing about them.

They had cups of hot chocolate. Gerry changed into a pair of felt slippers, finely checked trousers, a white shirt and string tie. He loved Allie with his eyes. Her excited relief and his excited satisfaction held each other off. They waited to relax to contentment before they spoke the things that wanted to be said.

Gerry said, "This is the way to come home. Just come. That's all."

They went to bed. Allie cried softly. Gerry was gentle. He couldn't get enough of her beauty. They whispered happy new year to each other many times. Gerry wondered why Allie called him Gerald and not Gerry. They whispered until early morning, then went to sleep.

Gerry is home.

I was at the first party Allie gave in the Queen's Hotel drawing-room. It was the day we got our first McLaughlin-Buick touring sedan. I was all morning taking the grease and heavy paper off the bumpers and polishing the brass. I worked hard at it because I wanted to try the car in the deep snow on the township roads before dark. It was the biggest car in town and I was proud of it.

It was Valentine's day – the first Valentine's day I had ever sent a card with a message on it that I meant. It was a fussy card, all paper lace around the edges, a picture of a curly-haired boy in blue trousers and checked jacket handing a message to a girl in a pink frock. There was an ivory-coloured postal delivery box between them. The poem was in gold ink and it glistened in the light when you moved the card slightly. Froody still has the card, she says.

It was seven weeks after Gerry got home. Everybody was there. I angle-parked the Buick beside the cast-iron hitching-post in front of the main entrance to the hotel. That made me feel good, but handing Froody down from the high car and holding her elbow on the way in made me feel better.

Allie was beautiful in her new drawing-room. Gerry was nervous most of the night and he laughed loudly with Froody when all the guests had settled themselves in groups.

Jeth Geddes was there, a little drunk. I heard him in the gents' room talking to a couple of fellows. He didn't see me. I heard him say, "Christ, that Allie's beautiful." I knew he wanted her badly. The kind of man he was, I didn't blame him.

Gerry and Allie stood inside the double doors and welcomed the guests. We were all there promptly. We had heard about the room and there'd never been a party in the hotel before. When we were all there, the doors were closed. We were isolated from the town so that any ideas of who we thought we were didn't mean anything any more.

Allie stood tall with her back to the doors, her hands still on the glass knobs. She looked around and saw we were obviously admiring her room.

I was on the other side in one of the window alcoves with the gold drapes behind me. I thought to myself it wouldn't hurt if I walked over to Allie and told her that I loved her. She was some older than me and it wouldn't matter, she wouldn't get huffy. Besides, I meant it. I was in love with Allie, in my way, the way Jeth was in his, and the way I assumed Gerry to be in his way. I knew there were people in the room who wouldn't love Allie in any way, but I wondered what it would be like if they all had ways of loving her and did. It made me kind of dizzy.

In my eyes it was like one of those vague impressionistic paintings where there are tiny dabs of colour and light, and everything sort of running together, held together. There was Allie in a black rustly gown with a white blouse top, her hair in tight, shining coils, two shiny silver combs in the back, but she didn't seem distinct. She sort of flowed into the grey doors and they sort of flowed her on into the red wallpaper and the cream ceiling so that it was all of a piece – Allie in her beautiful drawing-room, a proud hostess, me loving her, Jeth loving her, Gerry loving her, maybe others. I loved her and wanted to tell her. Outside of her husband, I thought, I'd be the only one with the guts to tell her, if I told her.

The party? It was a little stiff and shy at first because there were families held together in the room who never had anything to do with each other outside. As the night grew on, though, they had to have something to do with each other. Drifting around after Froody from group to group, I heard Allie saying "other things, not the private things necessarily, but what stops the loneliness. Do you know what I mean?"

The older people, ones with sons and daughters there, kept close together for some reason. Oh yes. Somebody sat down at the parlour organ and played Tosti's "Goodbye." Everybody laughed.

On the way home, Froody said to me, "It's certainly not the kind of thing that's happening everywhere else, but she's right, Dougie, isn't she?" It took me a few days to figure that out. My mother made me uncomfortable when she said Allie and her party and her drawing-room were kind of sweet and old-fashioned.

The day after the party I drove over to the Queen's. I angle-parked beside the hitching-post again and went in. Gerry was opening a big packing-case with a small wrecking bar. The case was in the middle of the lobby. Allie was on a stool by the clerk's desk.

"Oh dear, Gerald, isn't it a pity it wasn't here in time for last night?"

I reached over and prised out a board with my hand while Gerry loosened more nails with the wrecking bar. There was a chandelier in the packing-case. It was a big one. There must have been a thousand pieces. Each one was wrapped in white tissue paper.

Allie jumped down and unwrapped the first little package. She held the long crystal bead up in the air and made it zing by flicking her finger against it.

"It's beautiful, Gerald, just beautiful."

"Wait'll we get it up, Allie, then see."

The three of us carried handfuls of the wrapped pendants upstairs to the drawing-room. We shuttled back and forth, smiling to each other gravely as we passed. It happened when I was making my fifth or sixth trip. Allie was going up the stairs beside me. I looked at her, saw how she was concentrating on getting up the stairs safely, without stumbling or dropping any of the pendants. There was a wonderful happiness on her face.

"Allie," I said, "I'm in love with you."

"Dougie."

How she managed it, I'll never know, but when she said that one plain word, she scolded me for being impertinent and, at the same time, let me know she didn't think it was an impertinence. She thanked me, too, I thought, and acknowledged she knew what I meant.

"I only wanted you to know the way things are with me. There's no sense keeping these things secret, is there?"

"No sense at all." She agreed with me.

I followed her into the drawing-room. We put our packages down on the floor. She looked at me sternly.

"You're too young to be, well, you know what I mean, when you say that, and you're too old to be the other way. You're serious, aren't you?"

My throat felt terribly thick, but I was happy, the happiest I'd ever been, when she said that. I nodded.

"You're right. There's no reason to keep such things secret. No reason at all."

I was still remembering the way she said my name on the stairs.

She held up one of the longest of the crystal pendants. "This one will be yours, Doug. Remember, it's one of the longest ones."

Gerry came in. We smiled all around and I said, "Look, I almost forgot. I came in to tell you I appreciated being here at your party last night. It was something special and I'll not forget for a long time."

"Thank you, Dougie. We want you and Froody to come often," Allie said. Froody was not in my mind at the moment.

Allie and Gerry were down on the floor by now, arranging the bead things out in a glittering star pattern around the frame of the chandelier. I stepped back and looked at them. It was a good feeling. I backed away to the door.

"Call me when you have it ready to put up and I'll come help." I noticed that the long pendants were out on the edge of the pattern they made on the floor. I wanted to see how they looked with the chandelier up. I looked at them, then at Allie and went out.

I decided then that I'd never refuse an invitation to a party there. I never told Froody how I felt about Allie. She wouldn't have understood. That's why I'm not the one to be talking about those affairs. There I was wanting Froody so bad and this other quiet thing about Allie. Even if Allie was older than me, even if she was married, it seemed more right.

It seemed more right because it involved more than two people. There was one party later on that spring when Allie talked about love and respect. I asked her what she meant when she used the word love. She laughed with everybody there, but looked up at the chandelier for me only, and I knew.

At least I thought I had the idea that love for Allie was all tied up in her parties and with the chandelier glistening over them and one of the beads in the chandelier was mine. That was enough. That's as far as I ever got with it, anyway.

Alison lay dead upstairs. Only the doctor knew. Gerry came down to the lobby and called Doug Framingham on the phone.

"Hello, Dougie? It's Gerry. Look, could you come over? Right now?"

He shoved the telephone away and sat, waiting. A feeling for Alison: he pushed his memory back to before he went away, but couldn't remember what she was like then. That was it. Alison was so new the day he got back.

Doug Framingham came in. His faded Malacca cane hung on his forearm and he walked slowly to the chair in the big window bay facing on the street. The green blind was drawn, but the street light outside shone through the stained glass window and cast a soft fan of colours on the worn linoleum.

Gerry spoke at last. "You and I are getting old now, aren't we, Doug?"

"Not so much old as over the hump. We've stopped living and started dying. It's the easy way."

"Don't talk like that tonight, Doug. Tell me about the old days. Tell about your wedding day."

"What's wrong?"

"Alison's dead."

"Dead."

"And I can't remember what she was like before I went away at all. Can you?"

"When your father was alive, you used to sit with her on the earth dam below the pond. I remember the kids going to high school used to whisper about you."

"I can't remember that."

"There's no need to remember that far back." Now Doug Framingham's voice was full of a young gentleness that no one had heard for many years, a fresh loving gentleness that didn't belong to an olding man. But there it came in his voice and Gerry, trying hard to remember back, was grateful.

"There was a time when you borrowed my horse and rubber-tired buggy to take her driving after church."

"That wasn't really Alison was it? I can't remember back that far. It really began when I came back."

"What really began?"

Before he answered, Gerry considered his private discovery. Allie had not been the girl he left behind. She had been new and his memory of her at that time was something like his awareness of the tenderness in Doug's voice now.

"Don't you remember, Doug? The first party in the drawing-room? Helping us to put up the chandelier?"

It came back to them easily and swiftly. They stared at the darkened window, each wondering what the other knew.

"But what's the use of knowing," Gerry said. "Alison is dead and it's over now. It doesn't much matter when it started. It doesn't matter what she meant. She was going against the way the world was and it felt right to me and I helped her all I could, but it doesn't matter now."

"It does matter," Doug said. He felt like the boy-man again, helping to carry handfuls of crystal pendants up the stairs to the drawing-room.

"No, we're growing old and it doesn't matter. We're just making old noises."

"But don't you see? Now we have a right to. It matters to the new ones coming along to hear our noises."

So they sat and remembered on the night that Allie died. Each memory began with the chandelier. Memory came on memory until Gerry stood up suddenly.

"Stay there, I'll be right back."

Staring into the dark window, Doug followed in his mind where Gerry was going. Across the lobby, around the corner, up the stairs, his steps were audible. Then on the faded mulberry rug there was quiet. Doug heard no sounds in the time it took Gerry to get in the drawing-room. Then there was a succession of quick muffled shattering noises from far off.

Gerry came back.

"I had to do it that way," he whispered. "That wasn't the way she wanted it, but I had to. I cut it down and smashed it with the axe."

One loving, remembering voice flowed into the other. The chandelier was destroyed, so the thread of memory had been established and the two old men took turns remembering.

"I remember Allie in a pale green, rustly dress, her hair glowing bronzy-red, her cheeks just a little pink with excitement. Every party was exciting. She was all proud and gracious. Moving here and there among the guests. She was gay, light, serene, floating kind of, hoping her guests were her friends, hoping that her affection for them would be accepted and conscious.

"She'd visit with a group of men for a few moments, then over to the Butler sisters and then on to the group of older women.

"Yes, the old ones, with their sons and daughters there. They'd listen politely and answer politely, but they watched all the time.

"And Allie moving among them, hoping she made everybody feel the way she did: fresh and warm.

"I remember the drawing-room brightly lighted, full of her friends, and the chandelier up there, brightest of all, shining down from the centre of the ceiling. Shining down and drawing up to its crystal beads all of what they felt.

"Those were good times. Every Monday morning she'd go into the room alone, lower the chandelier on its chains and go over it, polishing every bead.

"I guess there were folks who often wondered why we kept on inviting them. Maybe, they said to themselves, maybe we amounted to something once, but times are changing and we can't keep up with those parties.

"It all changed slowly and if I had seen it happening I would have moved away, gotten right out of the hotel business. We'd have gotten along somehow."

The two men found themselves upstairs in the darkened room.

"Look at us now," Gerry said. He stood beside the skeleton of the chandelier as he spoke. The shattered pendants lay out in a grim star pattern that made old Doug wince as he realized for the first time what his sorrow was. "Look at us now. Sad and cold compared to those days when the wallpaper was rich, rich red and this chandelier was a complete and beautiful sparkling under the ceiling. It changed through to grey so slowly, I didn't see it. But Allie must have seen it happening. We were getting old, I guess, only I wouldn't believe it."

"No no," Doug interrupted, "it wasn't getting old. The parties just didn't seem the same after a while. Things happened to the people around town."

Memory came on memory. Each memory began with the chandelier. Each loving, remembering voice flowed into the other.

"It got so there were only four or five parties in a year.

"Then that antique dealer came through town one day and – that was about twelve years ago, I guess – and offered spot cash for the chandelier. Said he was looking over all the old, country hotels in this part of the province. He offered spot cash and she wouldn't take it. Said she'd see about it some time.

"And she kept on spending Monday mornings dusting the chandelier. It was no concern of mine.

"After the antique dealer was around, I remember a Monday night when Allie came to bed early and cried into her pillow. She thought I was asleep, but I heard the tears until it must have been two o'clock in the morning. I couldn't say anything to her next day. All I did was worry. That was the day I found one of the little beads from the chandelier lying on a window ledge in the lobby. I left it there. I had no idea how it came to be there. A few days went by. Then Jeth Geddes died.

"I told Allie that Jeth had died and she just looked a little surprised. That's all. Never said a word about Jeth. Never even wiped at her eyes. That was the strange part. She always carried on something terrible when somebody as close as Jeth died. She loved him in a way, but never said a word.

"She could have remembered when Jeth was considered the most eligible bachelor in town. How the Butler sisters tried so hard to get him. How he married Lita after all."

Gerry and Doug walked slowly the length of the mulberry rug and down the main stairs to the lobby again.

"I was sitting right here behind the desk when I told her about Jeth dying. She reached over, picked up the little bead and handed it to me. 'Take this down cellar and smash it before you come to dinner,' she said. I had an idea it had to be done and after I smashed the bead I wondered what the end would be.

"It happened that way again a second time about two months after Jeth was buried. She came out of the room one Monday noon, right in front of me here in the lobby, and put a long glass bead in the same place. That night she cried again.

She tried to hide it from me, but I heard and was getting an idea of what was happening. Well, a few days later, word came from that clinic in Minnesota that old man Butler was dead. Missy Butler phoned the news to Allie. Allie asked me if I had heard. I nodded. She looked at the long glass bead in the window, then at me. I smashed that bead too.

"That was eleven years ago, so there were quite a few gaps in the chandelier yesterday. It happened just that way again and again.

"Gosh, when she came to bed last night, she was as natural as you please, really her old self. She asked me if I thought I was henpecked. I said I didn't think so. She said I must be henpecked because I always did what she wanted me to do. Then she got into bed, turned out the light and I was dozing off, feeling pretty good.

"All of a sudden in the dark she said, 'Whatever you do, don't let any antique dealer have the chandelier.'

"'What made you think of that?' I asked.

"'Never mind, just make sure that antique dealer doesn't get it. That's all.'

"As she talked her voice grew faint. I turned the light on. She was fretting and weak. I put in a call for the doctor. When I got upstairs again, she said, 'Take it down carefully and put it out in the carriage shed. I can't bear to let anybody have it that doesn't know. I don't know what I'd have done without it.'"

SIX

The kissing man

A REAL GIBSON GIRL Froody was, before she got married. Think of the main street then: a blazing July sun draining the colour out of the buildings from the Queen's Hotel down to Geddes's dry-goods store. Then Froody comes around the corner at the Queen's. Graceful, elegant she walks, and cool. Cool black flowing skirt, finely pleated starched blouse, her hair done up and back in a neat, big pompadour with pearly shell combs.

She always used to wear white in summer, white starched blouses usually, with puffed sleeves and neat cuffs. Her skirts were dark, full-pleated and graceful, perfectly pressed. It was a pleasure to watch her walk down the street and into Geddes's store.

The men who hung around Weaver's barber shop across the street used to breathe a little heavier on purpose when they watched her. And they talked about her ears. It was a good thing she never heard about that or she'd have combed her hair differently and stopped all the nudging.

But the neatness of her was something different from being a Gibson girl. Maybe her mother insisted on the severe dark skirts and white blouses. Maybe her mother didn't realize Froody, in a get-up like that, was just what it took on a hot day to put gumption in a fellow.

Geddes's dry-goods was where she worked before she finally married Dougie Framingham. She waited on customers. She was good at it. Always polite, she addressed everybody as Mister or Missis, even though some of the customers were blood relatives of hers. It was Mr. Geddes's idea.

"Froody, you call everybody Mister or Missis," he said, "and they won't want to go and shop at the store down the street."

Froody was a dreamy girl. Sometimes it was a bother to her to keep her mind on the work. Usually she stood quietly in the narrow space between the two long mahogany showcases that ran the length of the store. When there were customers to wait on, she drifted from one to the other as easy as you please.

"Not many real people come into the store any more," she said once. "There are weeks and weeks when I'm completely alone. I never see the customers as the people I know around town. They are there, and they're not there, kind of; without faces if you know what I mean."

"I'm not very tall," she said, "but I get this feeling I'm high up and the customers move along in the aisles away down out of reach. And sometimes I'm so thankful for it because that's where I want them to stay."

Somehow she always knew when she should snap out of it and start to be polite the way Mr. Geddes wanted her.

"You see a person moving closer to you, or you sense it I guess when you are clerking in a store," she said, "then you reach for the face and then reach for the name. After that it's easy."

Froody never knew it, but she wasn't like that to her customers – without a face. Froody was what was young and what was full of hope. Froody was proper beauty and proper beauty was becoming rare in town these days. Rare for most everybody. The only time you saw proper beauty was when Alison and Gerry gave one of their big parties in the drawing-room of the Queen's. Froody went to them with Dougie Framingham, chaperoned by her mother and father of course.

Well, it was a Thursday in July, the slowest day of the week, the slowest month of the year. There were only about ten women in the store. It was getting on for five o'clock. The kissing man opened the front door carefully and stepped in.

Mrs. Muncey was standing alone with her back to one of the show-cases, staring at the swatches of fabric fanned out on the long table next the wall. Her feet hurt, you could tell, and strings of greying hair had come loose and straggled on her shoulders. Geddes's was her last stop after doing all the stores in the block. Muncey, of course, was taking it easy in the cool of Weaver's barber shop. Mrs. Muncey was so tired she didn't turn around to see who it was when the kissing man came in.

The kissing man looked at her back for a long time. Tears came to his eyes. Then he walked right up beside Mrs. Muncey.

"You poor woman." His voice was a whisper, all compassion. Then he bent close to her and kissed her full on the mouth. His fingers touched her elbow for a moment. He walked out of the store. Nobody saw.

Mrs. Muncey could feel the weight of her sagging and knew her grey hair was straggling. "No, it's not. It's not fair at all," she said. She held to the show-case for support a moment, worked her lips in and out, then left the store.

At the back, Froody wondered what had gotten into Mrs. Muncey, letting the door slam like that.

That was all there was to it on Thursday.

Saturday is always the big day at Geddes's. The following Saturday, Aunt Cress went into Geddes's with Miss Corvill, the librarian at the time. Aunt Cress said the store was something like the street dance the Lodge puts on every fall: people chattering easily, a bustling back and forth, people helloing each other a little more than usual. It was like this every Saturday. Froody and Mr. Geddes were busy making out bills, making change at the old wind-up cash register, talking a little faster.

Miss Corvill was a pleasant enough woman, shy, not many friends. Nobody knew much about her, except that she was a cracking good librarian. This day she got separated from Aunt Cress in all those bustling women, so she stood idly fingering the texture of the different cloths spread on the table.

She had to turn around. She would never be able to tell why. She just had to. The kissing man was there close to her. All in his face was pity. He took her hand firmly in his two. He pressed her palm to his cheek.

"Oh God," he whispered, "why does it have to come to this?" His voice trailed off. He dropped her hand.

Who lived once, and was a person to love, now is a wisp of loneliness. Why is it that order of living, loving and loneliness? Why do I see it wherever I go? I dream of taking you, Miss Corvill, and loving your body with my eyes, touching you, making you cry for shame until the shame is out of you, making you cry then for that, and giving it, giving it all. The way no man ever did. It's the beginning. The beginning of life and love. And it's the end. The end of loneliness that leaves you dust. Why do I see it wherever I go? Living, loving and loneliness.

He left the store.

"Let's go home, Cressie, I'm so worn out from shopping. The heat and all. Let's go home." She knew her pince-nez hid the tears.

Froody saw it happen and wanted to scream out. Miss Corvill didn't seem shocked, angry or surprised. Froody wanted to ask her what he had said, but she didn't dare.

After Miss Corvill and Aunt Cress left the store, Froody reached out for the faces in the crowded store because a change had come over everything. It was now a barren order-liness: everything in place, everyone concentrating on their purchases, no more voices of excitement or welcoming happiness as people met in the crowded aisles. The warmth had gone.

That Saturday night Froody stayed in her room after supper and cried. She wanted to know, to get it, to share. It was all so hopeless.

Dougie Framingham showed up that night, as usual, and Froody told her mother to tell him to go away, that she wasn't able to see him. Later she came downstairs and found her mother pressing her father's Lodge sash. Her eyes lighted up and she thought of telling her mother again to stop it, that the Lodge wasn't worth it, that there was nothing to those men getting together except a band of thin cotton across still chests. She said nothing, though, because she saw her mother knew what she wanted to say. Froody sat on the bottom step of the stairs and watched.

"Muncey, Weaver and Sobel, Muncey, Weaver and Sobel," she said to herself. "Muncey, Weaver and Sobel, say them over and over again and nothing happens." She frowned at her mother's back and at the sash on the ironing-board.

The name of Muncey reminded Froody of Mrs. Muncey the past Thursday, slamming the front door at the store. Then the memory of the kissing man with Miss Corvill was bursting in her and stayed with her while she went upstairs to bed and until she fell asleep.

Next day she watched for the kissing man at church and she watched for him as she and Dougie drove sedately out to the town line and back in his rubber-tired buggy. She never saw him.

Monday was another hot, humid day, so there weren't many people in the store. Poor Mr. Geddes was so uncomfortable. He was much too fat for his age and he sat uneasily in a wicker porch chair that squeaked under his bulk. He stationed himself close to the window so he could see who was out on the street.

Froody was waiting on Mrs. Lalling, the widow who was on town relief. Mrs. Lalling was made small and hushed by the rich store atmosphere: that comfortable clothy smell, the old shining mahogany. She didn't like Mr. Geddes to be sitting there while she bought the few yards of print she needed. The height of the ceiling was an aching reminder that she was poor and shouldn't be in such luxury. She was nervous when Froody left her to go to the back of the store for some cloth. She wanted to leave then and knew she should have left at that very moment but she couldn't make her legs move.

The kissing man came in. He went by Mr. Geddes, past the long table and stopped. He looked to the back of the store where Froody had gone. Then he made Mrs. Lalling turn around. He pressed her close to him. Mrs. Lalling cried softly and gently.

He crooned, "Don't cry, don't cry."

Stepping into a dead man's shoes for a while, the body in earth out beyond the Fair Grounds, and she sits weary home alone.

Mr. Geddes hoisted himself up out of the chair and came to Mrs. Lalling. The kissing man ran to the back of the store. He reached the store-room door as Froody came out. He stopped.

"Mrs. Lalling is crying, isn't she?" Froody asked.

"Yes she is, poor soul."

"Why didn't you come to me?"

He went past her, towards the back door. Froody felt cold order coming on and the feeling of people without faces. She knew she would never see him again after this.

"You've been one of the lucky ones," he called back to her. "You haven't needed me yet."

She knew more then than she wanted to know, ever.

?

SEVEN

A leaf for everything good

IN THOSE DAYS there was a deep pond where the bowling greens are now. It was formed by an earth dam that had been built to make the fall for the water-power mill. The big willow, there, put its branches out over the pond and dropped its leaves into the water every autumn.

Men in work boots, young men in copper-toed boots, bare-footed boys and girls and, later on, bicycles, firmed the earth down around the edge of the pond and made a cool walk that began at the mill and went upstream to the foot-bridge, then downstream to the shadows under the willow tree.

The mill pond was a place to go, because there came the water from springs far up country, water that flowed in long curves through the low meadow-land and into the town where it was used by the mill before it turned west for the lake. If a man's troubles were not taken away downstream with the water that had to go that way, they were at least cooled by September breezes as he sat on the earth dam or as he dangled his feet in the water at the overflow gate.

The old man got the shape of the town clear in his heart by coming to the pond every Sunday and by walking once or maybe twice around the path, then resting under the willow. When he got too old to work, he took to spending all his afternoons on the banks of the pond, in the sun on cool days, in the shade when it was warm.

The continuation school in those days was just beyond the pond. Kids who lived in this end of the town naturally walked across the earth dam going to and coming home from school.

The first-form kids were nervous about him. He sat with his back against the willow, watching. The first-form kids whispered to each other after they had passed safely over the earth dam and by the old man. The ones who knew everything (there were always some in each new year) told the others it was only the old man who sat under the willow tree by the mill pond. He had always been there. He was too old to work. That's how the old man knew whose children were at school.

Finn was the only boy who stopped to talk to the old man.

"You'll be late for school, boy. She's rung the first bell."

"You be here after school?"

"Aren't I always? I'll be here."

That afternoon, Finn sat down on the grass, facing the old man.

"What did you learn today, son?"

"I didn't learn nothing. Don't you know who I am? I'm Finn, the dumbest first-former she ever had."

"I know who you are, all right. What's the matter? Don't you like school? Your maw certainly did."

"I got other things on my mind. Did you know my mother?"

"I knew her. I'll tell you about her. What have you got on your mind?"

"Oh, things. I don't know. I don't put my mind to algebra or anything like that."

The days went by, the way they do for a boy in school. Finn stopped nearly every day for a visit with the old man. On the days when he stopped to count milk bottles rattling into the steam cabinet at the dairy, he remembered to tell the old man, on the way by, that he would stop for a while after school, if she didn't keep him in.

One day the old man said to him, "You don't hang much with the other kids. What's the matter? You too quiet for them?"

"No, they laugh at me for being dumb in school. I don't mind. I make out all right."

"How'd you like to learn something they'll never know?"

"What about?"

"You see me sitting here every morning when you go to school, don't you? And you see me still here when school's out. I guess I should know something about this pond by now, eh?"

"I guess so."

"Take this willow tree. It was here before the town was. Look at those branches reaching up there. Think of what you could see if you could sit on the highest one. Under us, the roots go down and spread out all over, under the pond, under the school-yard. This willow is busy taking from the air, taking from the earth, taking what it needs, taking all the things we don't know but that travel in the earth and in the air. The love that's in an up-country man that can't be expressed. It's got to go somewhere. Maybe it goes in the air and is taken by this willow. The tears of a lonely girl who wants a friend. She might come and sit under this tree and cry her tears into the roots.

"What about the regrets of a father who never got to love a son who went away to die in a war? He'd come here to be alone. These leaves hold that. The remorse of a boy alone here in the dark with his girl. The compassion of an old man who knows he is going to outlive his wife."

"But the leaves fall into the water in October," Finn whispered.

"Yes. A leaf of love, a leaf of loneliness, a leaf of regret, a leaf of remorse, a leaf of compassion, a leaf for everything good and forgotten, for everything bad and always here. They fall into the pond and the trout eat them."

"The trout?"

"Sure. There are trout in the pond, son. Everybody in town thinks the trout have gone, but the big ones are still here in the pond. You've got to be patient to see them. That's all."

"I thought the pond was fished out long ago."

"This pond is never fished out. Look at it. A widening. Holding the water that comes down the creek, holding it back for a few minutes, then letting it through the mill-wheel and down the race and going on. That's what's important. Going on because it must. But here in the widening the pond catches all that falls from the willow and the trout eat it. The fish are there now, taking from what's upstream, staying here at the widening, taking from the tree, avoiding the lures, living, living."

"Do you believe that?" Finn got up to go.

"Believe? I know." It was a week before Finn spoke to the old man again.

Finn made himself go back and talk to the old man again because he saw that he was the only one who would. Besides the old man did not always talk as strangely as he did the last time. He was a friend, kind of, except for that.

He wondered what the old man was driving at. He worried a little, because he had said he knew Finn's mother. Maybe he was an old family friend of some kind. Maybe he was in cahoots with the teacher, the way the young doctor at the hospital was. He'd have to be careful. But there were the trout. He ought to know. Trout in the pond.

He slid down the dry clay by the iron bridge and over to the earth dam. He looked across and saw the old man was there. From that distance, the old man looked more shapeless than usual, huddled up and still.

"Hello there, son. Haven't seen you for a few days."

"Oh, I was going to school by the post office and the foot-bridge the past while."

"Kind of a change, eh?"

Finn noticed then the old man had a loosely woven robe wrapped around his shoulders under the faded blue smock coat.

"Say, have you been sick?"

The old man squirmed a little to shift the robe off his neck. "No, not exactly sick. Just getting on I guess."

"Maybe you shouldn't be sitting down here. The air is still kind of swampy."

The old man was impatient with Finn's concern. "You doing any better at school?"

"Same as usual, I guess. I don't expect I'll pass. Paw'll probably put me to work in the axe-handle factory this July if I fail."

"Your mother wouldn't have liked that."

"How come you knew my mother?"

"I happened to make a point of getting to know her when she got married, but nothing came of it. Your dad is a pretty sullen man, take him any way you care to."

In a way Finn wanted the old man to go on talking about his mother, but he was afraid if he did he'd not get to talking some more about the trout, so Finn interrupted.

"Uh, these trout. You think they'd be good eating?"

"Best eating in the world. That's if you could catch one."

The boy turned directly towards the old man. "Do you think I could?"

"Knowing your mother, I'd say yes. Knowing your father, I'm not so sure."

The boy couldn't figure out how his mother and father could have anything to do with catching trout. "What do you mean?"

"I mean the trout are for special people. They are not ordinary trout, you know. I explained that."

"Wouldn't they rise to a coachman?"

"I doubt it."

"A worm?"

"Not a chance."

"What, then?"

"Patience, maybe. And a kind of strength you're too young to understand yet."

"Maybe I understand more than you think I do."

"What do you understand?"

"You are an old friend of my mother's and you know that I don't get along so good in school and this whole trout business is a way you've got of telling me if I don't work better at school and if I don't make friends with the kids, you won't tell me how to catch the trout. If there are any."

"Is that all?"

Finn was excited and disappointed. He was afraid it was true and he was ashamed of the good times he had talking to the old man. He turned his head away and looked at the pond.

"I don't know."

"Well, maybe you better go away and try and figure out what I'm all about. Try and remember if you ever saw me talking to any of the other ones. Think about them for a while. Come and talk to me about it whenever you feel like it."

So Finn got up and went back up to the main street and along the store fronts and past the rink until he came to the blacksmith's shop. He stood in the doorway and watched for a few minutes but it didn't seem to matter, so he went home and lay on his bed and cried.

He avoided the pond and the willow tree again until the thought came to him that the old man was maybe not interested in his school work, but wondered what Finn was to do when he got out of school. What he had said that day he talked about the trout hadn't much to do with a boy, more for grown-ups. Maybe that was it.

He ran across the school-yard and down to the willow tree.

"Tell me again. Tell me about the tree and what it does and the river and a man's troubles. Tell me again so I can understand."

He called it as he came near the willow tree and the trunk of it was a pure cold grey and the leaves were a shivering green and the pond was a soft shiny black. The shade seemed a little damp. The old man was not there.

He ran up to the road, across the iron bridge and on to the main street. At Geddes's corner, where there were men sitting under the awning, he called out.

"Where is he? The old man who sits under the willow tree. Where is he?" And they looked down at him and said nothing and Finn wondered what there was about them to make them feel so proud of themselves. "Where is he?" he asked finally. They looked at each other and smiled a little.

Finn ran on. He ran across the street and down to the Queen's Hotel. There were men standing beside the hitching-post. "Where is he? Where does the old man live who sits under the willow tree?"

One of the men swept Finn up by the elbows and held him in the air, close to his red face.

"He lives in a cave and he'll eat you if you go near him."

The others laughed and Finn squirmed away from the red-faced one and ran catty-corner across to the bank. There was no one to ask. Maybe he was sick. He ran down the tunnel of oaks towards the hospital. His legs felt light and strong and he thought he would keep running until he found the old man, but he slowed down to a walk on the cinder path into the hospital.

The young doctor told him the old man was dead.

"But he promised to tell me something."

"Was he a relation of yours, sonny?"

"Are you sure he's dead?"

"I'm sorry. He's dead."

There was no feeling at the old man's funeral. It was one of those days when the sun was so clear it took the colour out of the leaves of the trees that shaded the street and left the church warm and dark and unfriendly. No branch moved and there was no sound, not even the bell. The sky was high and blue and the town lay dwarfed under it and they were going to bury the old man who didn't get a chance to speak to Finn again.

At the funeral, Finn said to himself it would have been all right to have gone to school by the dam those days he was avoiding the old man. He couldn't have said anything to hurt him. It was just that the old man knew. Finn wanted to know and the old man hinted and Finn was ashamed the hint wasn't enough. He watched the democrat with its grey canopy and velvet rope go down the street on the Fair Grounds road, down to where the cemetery was.

He came back this way towards home. He met his father at the corner and they walked together. Finn noticed the varnish stains were like ugly freckles on his father's hairy hands.

"You in school today?"

"I went to the old man's funeral. They buried the old man today."

"You skipped school for that?"

"They let me go. It doesn't matter."

"I thought you didn't like funerals."

"This was different. He knew maw, he said. Got to know her when you and she were married."

"Crazy. Crazy in the head."

"He was all right. We talked quite a bit together. He liked to talk to me."

"High time he died. Been sitting down in that swamp for as long as anybody can remember. Crazy in the head."

gossip

"He made sense. At least he'd've made sense to older people. Sometimes I didn't understand what he was driving at."

"Like you don't understand what that school is driving at, I suppose. You'd understand if you paid attention sometimes."

"I guess so. I guess that's right."

They were in the house then. It was dark, hot, and smelled of old cooked cabbage.

"And another thing mister, now that we're in the house, you'll ask me before you go to another funeral. I suppose you thought you'd sneak off to this one and me not know, eh?" The father <u>hit Finn on the side of the head</u>. Finn backed away.

"I didn't sneak anywhere. I told you where I was. I didn't try to hide anything."

"No back talk." <u>He hit Finn again.</u> "Get in the kitchen and get to work."

So Finn began to fish in the pond every morning before school. Naturally everybody laughed at him and asked him what he expected to catch.

Wouldn't you know? they asked. He's in a daze half the time at school. Never passes a term test. Can't answer a question. Stands around day-dreaming at the dairy or the blacksmith's shop. Wouldn't you know? <u>With a father like that it's no wonder.</u>✳

Others were kind and wished that someone would go gently to Finn and lead him away from the pond and explain to him that the fish had gone long ago. But there was no one gentle left in the town to do it. So the kind ones felt uncomfortable and hoped it wouldn't last for long.

He started off by using a cheap, store-bought royal coachman fly on a silk leader. In a few mornings he became expert at dropping the fly onto the surface of the water where he wanted it to go. Nothing happened, except that he became aware of the slight movement of the water in the direction of the earth dam. He never noticed that before.

When he changed from artificial flies to worms, he noticed that it was possible to see only part way into the water, that the worm dropped into it and soon disappeared. The odd leaf dropped from the willow tree and drifted along with the water to the dam, but he never got a bite.

Why does he stay at it so long? they asked. For goodness' sake, somebody tell him, they said. <u>And the kind ones began to worry for Finn</u>.

Once a third-form boy sneaked up behind him and pushed him towards the water. Finn's feet were soaked and he went to his knees in the clay mud. He had to go home and change.

Another time he was fishing from the overflow gate and lost track of the time. It was getting on for nine when the school kids tramped heavily across the gate, making it shiver. Finn held on to the top board with his fingers and held his fishing-rod between his knees until they had all passed. They stood on the other side of the pond and laughed at him.

All the excitement of getting the Fair Grounds ready for the Dominion Day races didn't stop him. Neither did the final examinations at school. He was at the pond every morning at seven o'clock, trying every kind of bait. He never got a bite.

Examination results were to be pinned on the big bulletin board outside the principal's office on the last day of June. Finn knew what to expect there and knew what to expect when he took his report card home to his father. He kept on fishing.

That last school morning was a solemn one. The sun rose a glaring yellow through a dank, low mist back of the school. The little river mists spiralled up and disappeared. Finn was quiet, standing on the dam, his line making swishing noises through the air. The old willow drooped in the morning stillness and the picture of its roots the way the old man described them came to Finn. He could feel them under him and he could feel the process of taking from the earth. He saw a girl sitting under the willow, crying, and if he closed his eyes he could see her tears falling on the clay. He looked up and saw the top branches and it came back to him. He heard a noise behind him. He turned and saw the kids had started coming to school.

He reeled in his line, pressed the hook into the cork handle of the rod, tucked it under his arm and ran off to school.

There was an assembly of all the pupils in the school. The principal spoke and no one tittered or scuffled in their seats. Finn paid no attention. He wanted to get it over with. Everybody knew that one of the teachers was outside the room, pinning the results up. Everybody knew the classes would file out one at a time and go by the board and look for their names. Everybody knew what was to happen. Finn wanted to get it over with.

The principal's talk droned on. She couldn't speak very clearly and she had a lot to say. Finn supposed she would have something to say, not directly of course, about him. He didn't care.

The third-formers got up and lined up along the front, then shuffled out the door to go by the board. As the last of the third-formers went out, the second form got up. Finally the first-formers went out. Finn was last in line. His name wasn't on the list.

He went into the classroom. The clock said five minutes to twelve. Finn gathered up his books without sitting down. The teacher asked what he thought he was doing.

"I expect I'm going home now," he said and went out the door. The others laughed uneasily.

He went by the bulletin board and looked again. His name was not there. He looked to make sure he was in front of the right list, then went out the door of the school, looked for a moment at the pond across the yard, then ran for the road as fast as he could go. He would beat his father home.

His father didn't come home for lunch that day. He probably stayed at the factory and ate a pick-up lunch from the café across the street.

Finn was disappointed that he couldn't get it all over with. He ate what there was at home, then picked up his fishing-rod and went to the pond. He sat quietly in the shade of the willow and cast the line into the pool regularly. When the whistle at the factory blew, Finn went home.

His father was there on the porch, waiting.

"Well?"

"I failed. My name wasn't on the list."

"I guess you know what that means."

"I guess you want me to start in at the factory."

"You're bloody right I do, you lazy little slut. I found out about you at noon today and you're to see Mister Penny at the horse barns tomorrow at one-thirty. And you'll be there, too."

"All right. I'll be there."

"And I'll be watching for you."

Dominion Day had a fair and promising morning that year. Nobody remembers it for that, though. Nobody except Finn. He was up as usual to get his father's breakfast. They didn't speak. His father went off to handle Mr. Penny's horse entered in the 2.28 at the track. As soon as he was around the corner, Finn set out for the pool. It was a good day.

Everybody was at the races, so no one saw or thought of Finn. About noon-time when things started to pick up at the Fair Grounds, Finn's father watched for him. He thought the boy would be around to see the horses warm up. There was no sign of him.

"Boy didn't show up, heh?" Mr. Penny said at a quarter to two.

After the races were all over and after the horses were in their vans on their way up county for the meet there next day, Finn's father came to the pool, looking for him. It was still light, but the shadows were long. He wondered if Finn might have fallen into the pond. He walked around the trampled path, went across the foot-bridge and down under the willow tree.

He found Finn's rod there and a grey old trout that measured nearly thirty-four inches long.

Later that night Emerson told him Finn got on the one-twenty flag-down.

EIGHT

The man who lived out loud

THE MAN WHO LIVED out loud didn't last very long. He came to town during the bad year. He came out from the city, or wherever he was from, on the flag-down. He stepped down to the platform, walked a couple of steps towards the station, then let his suitcase drop on purpose. There was a smart-alec bend to his elbow when he did it. Then he looked at the station and laughed a big, noisy laugh that he didn't seem to want to stop.

<u>Nobody in town knew him.</u> Nobody was at the station to meet him. He acted as though he was glad to be there and he hoped there was somebody inside the station watching him.

He had a real name all right. John something. It's sure to be on the desk pad at the Queen's. Nobody used it.

It was too bad he came in the bad year. There was enough sorrow in one year to do a town for ten. It was the year Doc Fletcher died so suddenly. It was the year Hazel what's-her-name made a mess of her marriage and had to come home. That's Frank Allerton's girl. It was the year Marty's uncle Jeth dropped dead in a snow bank four days after he bought a big insurance policy. There was a lot of big sorrow like that. Even the weather was against the town. Rain all three days of the County Fair. No snow for Christmas. The creek flooded bad in the spring.

The man who lived out loud soon got into the habit of going to Weaver's barber shop every day around lunch time. He got to know and was good friends with quite a few people. He visited around. He helped with the gardening, repairing, odd-jobbing, whatever was doing. At the end of three months he could mosey into almost any back yard or up onto any front porch in town to sit and talk.

One day when he was sitting in Weaver's, the boys were talking about this and that. There was an easy kind of feeling in the shop. Weaver was subdued. The others slumped in chairs and didn't move or talk much: just a few words to agree or disagree, or a grunt of pleasure, or a knowing sniff. But the man who lived out loud sat straight up in his chair. His eyes moved from one to another quickly.

"What do you think boys, you've been around the map, ain't this the best by our lady town in the world? I've never seen anything like it in all my born days," he said.

There was quiet and a chair squeaked. Nobody said anything.

"Well ain't it?" he asked. "You all live here. You're happy. What about it?"

Muncey looked at him with a dull squint on his face and said, "I guess you lived a lot of places in your day. How come you light here?"

"That don't matter. I ain't a part of the town yet. I just come here and it's got a good feeling and I want to hear about it from you. You've all been here all your lives, I bet. I bet you wouldn't trade places with anybody."

"We aren't talkers like you," Muncey said. "We just sort of feel things, grow up with things and there's all there is to it."

"What things?" he asked, leaning at Muncey. "What things are just there?"

That was when Doctor Fletcher stuck his head in the shop door and said, "You'd save a lot of Lodge postage if you'd stop sending me those application blanks, Weaver. Why don't you give up?"

The doctor shut the door quickly before Weaver could answer. The man who lived out loud jumped up and went out after the doctor. He caught up to him along by the hotel.

"I like this town, Doc. The people are fine. Seem to have started out with clean ideas, but they sure don't want to let a fellow get too close to them. Know what I mean? What do you figure? They think I'm going to mess things up if I get inside their lives a little? I don't mean anything. What happened to them anyway?"

The doctor laughed and said, "It's all a question of diet. Maybe yours is a little rich just now. Taper off a little and you'll get along fine."

After Doctor Fletcher died so suddenly, the man who lived out loud was one of the first to drop in on the Doc's sister-in-law who moved into the Fletcher house after the funeral.

"You know, Missis Fletcher, I'm glad you come to this town, because now I ain't the biggest stranger. You're gonna love this town. I only been here a few months, but it's getting to be as much my town as anybody's now."

"Is there a lot of suffering here, Mister ah, I mean sickness and family sorrow, that kind of suffering? I've been here a few weeks now and I've heard some strange things about my brother-in-law. I think maybe he couldn't stand all the suffering and died. Like that. People say he was in the best of health before he died and they couldn't understand. Oh, we're born to suffer, I know, but I did hope this would be a refuge for me and Neddy."

"Born to suffer? Refuge? Missis Fletcher, you sound to me like one of those original-sin, vale-of-tears women. What kind of talk is that? You only around forty-five, I should judge, Missis Fletcher, and you are full of that born-to-suffer stuff. Let me tell you something. It's all poppycock. Know who thinks them things up? Guys who was too lazy for living."

"I won't have you shouting at me on my property," she answered.

"I have to shout to be heard, apparently, Missis Fletcher."

"Then I'm going inside." She closed the door on him.

He was tired when he got back to the lobby of the Queen's Hotel where he lived. Missy Butler was there and the man who lived out loud told her what he had said and what Mrs. Fletcher had said.

"Yes, yes. It's all so true. Things can be sad, but it's not right to think everything's sad from the word go. That's one of the fraileries of mankind, young man. Yes, certainly one of the fraileries."

The man who lived out loud said, "You're a good woman, Missy Butler, a good woman all right."

It was shortly after that when Hazel what's-her-name, Frank Allerton's girl, came home. The reason the man who lived out loud happened to be at the station was because the boys at Weaver's barber shop got tired of him and pestered him so he had to leave. He took to hanging around the freight sheds with Wes and the others there.

Hazel stepped off the train and the next thing she knew he was in front of her.

"You're in some kind of trouble, Missis Hazel. I don't know what your married name is, but you're an Allerton all right, and I aim to take your bags for you and walk them home for you."

He took the two travelling-bags and started walking towards the street. She came on beside him.

"Who are you? How do you know I'm in trouble?"

"Your daddy and I are kind of friends, Missis Hazel, and, mind you, he never told me one thing, but I knew, somehow, he was worried about you these past few days, so I kind of looked out for you to come. This is where you should come when you're in trouble. That's what a family is, you know. A family's to get rid of trouble as fast as it can."

They walked along a block.

"You're crazy. That's not what a family's for at all. I wish I could die."

"Now look, Missis Hazel, you're too young to be saying things like that. You're gonna get to like the idea and then you'll be done for. It gets bigger all the time and pretty soon it happens. Only it's slow and lonely. Big thing about God, Missis Hazel, he never tell you when you stop living and start dying. Look at it that way and you get a lot extra licks in living. Dying come along and you don't mind so much because it's a surprise. You see, everything is living and dying, first one, then the other. Trouble with a lot of folks, dying's easier, that's all."

He put her bags on the Allerton front porch. "You better try and make it work out, Missis Hazel."

That night, Frank Allerton let him have it. "You nosy parker," Frank yelled, "you keep to hell out of other people's affairs from now on. My little girl come home fit to be tied – you pushing your nose where it don't belong. You stay away, you hear?" Frank felt pretty proud of himself after that.

The next morning, the man who lived out loud was down at the freight shed. He and Wes hunkered down in the shade for a roll-your-own.

"You know, John, I got a sister. She's twenty-nine and she'll never get married. Ever think about people like that?" Wes worked his shoulder-blades against each other comfortably.

"What's wrong with her?"

"Nothing." Wes's voice squeaked as it usually did when he was uncertain. "She's a good cook. Not bad looking. Her legs aren't fat or anything. She still has ankles. Her bust's flat, I guess, but that don't mean be-all. Finished high school. She's smart."

"Maybe she didn't ever want to get married."

"That's all she does want. She wants a man, the worst way."

"I mean maybe she didn't want a man when she was ripe, you know what I mean."

"Listen, there've been guys coming around, sitting on the porch, waiting out the old lady, so they could muzzle up to Janey all over the sofa. One after another. But they kept going away. There wasn't one that seemed to want her bad."

"She feeling sorry for herself?"

"Not so much sorry for herself as mad at everybody. She gets mad at me for not bringing the boys from the freight shed over. She keeps saying old Butler up on the hill, with all his money, should be throwing parties every week so she could meet some men."

"I'll have to think some about it, Wes. See you later."

That day, Janey stopped writing letters to herself. That was how bad off she was, writing letters to herself. Mornings, she waited until her mother was out of the house, on her way to the store. Janey went straight to the library table, pushed the geranium back, and sat writing. It came fast and easy to her. She never stopped to blot. When her mother came back, Janey would be in the kitchen with an apron on, going at the dishes, humming as gay as you please. Her mother just looked.

Nights, Janey would go sad again and she'd ask Wes if anybody new came to town that day.

"What's the matter with that old Butler anyway," she'd say. "Lord knows he's got the money, and the house and all. You'd think he might throw a party or two so we could have a look around."

In her bedroom, she was careful to brush her hair, clean her nails and rub a glow into her cheeks. She always went to bed with the light out, so that the crinkle noise of the letter would make her sit up, turn the light on again and read what she had written that morning.

There it was: her own writing, often three sheets of it. She would read part way through, then throw the paper on the floor and weep.

It was the man who lived out loud who put a stop to it.

Now, Janey was a big, loose-built girl, something like Wes. When she took to skipping downstairs mornings, her mother knew something was in the wind, so she took to staying up later nights to see if maybe there was a fellow coming around regular after Janey.

"Keep an eye on her, Wes," she said. "There's something up." But Wes saw nothing, heard nothing.

"Oh, Mummy, I could sing all day," Janey said one morning.

"What's going on around here? You been fiddle-faddling around here these last few weeks like a randy dog."

"I've been somebody the last while. Not just plain old Jane. I've been somebody and I'm going to keep on for a long time. You wouldn't understand, maybe, I guess."

"Who you been horsing around with?" her mother shouted. "You been bobtailing around with somebody nights and I don't know about him. Who is it?"

"Nobody, Mummy. There's been nobody. Wes'll tell you. He's been watching all along the way you told him to."

Her mother slammed the kitchen door behind her as she went out.

At lunch time Wes came in. Janey was standing with her legs wide apart in the bay window that faced on the garden. From there she could see the tracks and the station on the other side. She didn't move when Wes came in and slumped down in the arm-chair.

"Mummy told you to watch me, didn't she Wes?"

"Yep."

"Well for God's sake, leave me alone. I'm sick of it. If anything happens, I'll let you know. All about it."

The way she stood, like a lady trick rider in the circus, Wes was timid. He didn't answer.

"It's crazy for Mummy to ask you to find out something. She could do a better job of it herself if she put her mind to it."

This was all passed on to her mother, later. But by now Wes was ashamed and didn't want to have anything more to do with it.

"Put my mind to it, eh?" Janey's mother laughed.

After lunch, Janey lit a cigarette. Wes sat on the front porch alone. The mother sat in the arm-chair, staring out the window. There was no sound.

Then the mother saw Janey appear in the garden and she watched her walk down the garden to the high-board fence that separated their lot from the railway tracks. It didn't mean anything. Probably going to sit in the gap of the fence and watch the two noon trains go by. Nothing in that.

Once settled in the fence gap, Janey told herself again that she would leave this house, leave her mother. The easy way would be to shake it off by getting married to somebody, anybody and start a home of her own. But she told herself it had to be destroyed before she started her family. That was what was right.

Crouched there, half hidden by the rhubarb that grew close to the fence, only her back visible from the bay window, Janey didn't know what she was watching, but she came there every day. What she came to see was a man and it was the man who lived out loud only she didn't know that or anything about him. And she dared not ask Wes about him. He knew who she was. That was why he was there on the other side of the tracks every day.

Two railway tracks separated her world from his. The tracks silvered off to the north and disappeared into the shallow cut where the township began. They curled into the town from the south, widening as they came into the four steel threads that kept her world from his.

He appeared from behind the freight shed every day at the same time, a few minutes before the north-bound train pulled in. He sat on the wide cement window ledge of the station. His hands were in his pockets. His head was bowed as though by sadness or thinking.

After the north-bound came to a stop, Janey could see his legs in the space between the tracks and the bottoms of the coaches. Each day the legs moved along the platform to the baggage car where he stood for a minute, then the legs moved down the length of the train to the last car. There he stood, waiting for the train to go. As it pulled away towards the cut in the distance, he watched. Then, after the engineer had blown for the level crossing, the man who lived out loud kissed his fingers, blew on them in the direction of the disappearing train and laughed loudly.

"And when he does that, a part of it all seems to go with the train," Janey said to herself each day.

Wes and the man who lived out loud got together for a smoke behind the freight shed one day that week.

"How's your sister these days Wes? Remember telling me about her a while back? She still sore at the world?"

"I'll tell you something funny," Wes said. "She isn't the least bit interested in a husband ever since that day I told you about her. I don't know what's got into her lately. She's happy and doesn't give a toot for anything. Maybe she's resigned to it now."

"You aren't very close to her, are you Wes?"

"Well, she's my sister."

"But she doesn't talk much about it to you, though. A husband I mean."

That night at dinner time, Wes crossed the tracks, crawled through the gap in the fence, went up the garden, and found

Janey waiting for him on the back porch. She was the way she always had been, before.

"Wes, that fellow you were sitting talking to this afternoon, what does he do? I mean, not his job or anything. But what's he like?"

She burst into crying and ran back into the house. Her mother smiled as Janey went by her into the bedroom. It was all over.

Wes told the man who lived out loud about it.

"Yes, of course, she saw you with me. You crossed the tracks for dinner the way you always do. She was expecting you. You know, Wes, living the way I do takes an awful lot out of a man. I'm terribly tired. It just can't be done. Either way it turns out bad, I guess."

That would have been the end of it all as far as Janey was concerned, except that Wes got a promotion to a clerking job inside the freight office. That meant he could get married. One of his first callers after the wedding was the man who lived out loud.

"Now that you've been away from your mother's place for a while, I figure I can tell you something I couldn't tell when your sister had that trouble." He waited.

Wes understood.

"Janey was afraid she was going to turn out like her mother. That was all."

"Would that be bad?"

"Sons aren't the judge of that, Wes, but daughters sometimes are. Janey didn't want it to happen. Still doesn't want it to happen. I tried to help her that time. I let her in on my life."

"Oh. It was you, was it?" Wes's voice squeaked. He made a grab for the man who lived out loud.

"Wait a minute, let me finish," he said, trying to hold Wes's shaking arms still. "The mistake was letting Janey see you and me together. She thought she was doing it all by herself, but you connected her life with mine too early. That took the mystery away and everything went ordinary again. She was on to the way I do it, but you crossed the tracks from me to her and that broke the direction. That was when she wanted to put her troubles directly on me. But that's out of the question, the way I've been feeling the last year. Out of the question."

Wes dropped his hands away from the man's jacket. The man who lived out loud politely said good night to Wes's bride, patted Wes on the arm, smiled a little, went out the front door, down the street to the Queen's Hotel, upstairs to his room where he wrote a short note, laid down on the bed and died.

The note read: The fraileries got too much for me. I didn't think it would be time to start dying so early. I guess the ones that live like me just can't keep it up.

NINE

What do the children mean?

H<small>E GRUMBLED OUT LOUD</small> as he walked. He had to walk to town, scuffing his boots through the rough gravel, breathing dust when a rig passed, stopping every forty rods or so to wipe the damp off his face. Kith offered to drive him but he laughed that gentle, looking-down laugh of his and said he'd walk.

(Kith was his daughter-in-law. She married young Tom that year barley went up to a dollar a bushel. She was a Sparling.)

So he materialized, out of the base-line road where he lived, on the eighth concession. (You don't see much traffic on that base-line road nowadays. Drive down the eighth some day and when you get to the base-line corner look over to your right towards the far greenery. That's the deep-cut creek valley. Old Johnson Mender used to live in there. That's all. It's an abandoned side road now.)

Old and alive he was as he walked. Up his road, under his sky. His sky that started up from the fingery little poplars, misty and blue two concessions away, and curved up over the eighth and down to the gently rising land where the township ends. His sky holding his world.

Grey hair perched out from under his straw hat in tufts. There was the leather look to his face, but his cheeks were pink warm. In under the shaggy brows, his eyes moved easily. They were old eyes but they weren't washed out yet.

The last time he had been to town was many years ago. Now it looked strange, bare and freshly painted. He kept his eyes straight ahead as he went by the blacksmith's shop, closed up now, and the harness shop that had been turned into an implement agency since he saw it last.

He remembered that the place where he was going was catty-corner with the bank and directly across from the Queen's Hotel. They'd changed the front quite a bit in sixteen years: slat blinds in the windows facing the street, so you couldn't see in any more. The glass door had new gold lettering that told the office hours.

He made the door shiver when he stepped in from the street. Inside it was too quiet, that was what was wrong. He wanted to get used to it, so he looked all around slowly. When he got to the wicket, it was easy for the clerk to tell he was hot and blustery, probably mad.

"Look here, young man," Mr. Mender started, the words rattling on each other as he spoke against the quiet, "I want three beautiful children. I want to take them with me. They must be young, full of spirit, and ready to do what I tell them."

The clerk settled himself on the high stool, leaning forward on his elbows on the counter. He tilted his head a little to one side before he spoke. One of those cantankerous old know-alls. Thinks we'll jump when he barks, does he? The clerk used his voice to cut and mock Mr. Mender.

"You're rather old to be asking for three children, aren't you, sir?"

"Rather old!" exclaimed the old man. "Listen you, I'm Johnson Mender. I'm the only man in this township with the right to ask for any children. You young whelp! Get out your order book and take my name and address and no back talk. That's the way this place was run not so many years ago."

The clerk's face went pink and he was angry with himself.

He couldn't catch a hold on the words to hurt and still this old man. He backed out of the cage and called for the manager.

The manager came and looked. His eyes went wide, then he smiled. He took Mr. Mender's arm and, together, they walked through the gate that kept customers separated from the business side of the office. In the manager's private room, Mr. Mender sat uneasily. The clay-splotched overalls and patched smock he had on were what you usually saw across the desk from the manager sixteen years ago, but they didn't seem right that day.

"It's been a long time since you were here, Mister Mender. About sixteen years, I should judge." The manager, Mr. Mender decided then, had a grocer-man's face, round, red and smooth; the kind of face that sticks to the job and hides whatever's inside. The old man remembered back, too, and smiled.

"Yes, yes, sixteen years ago this summer. But about my order to that clerk. I have to hurry home and get started."

"Hold on, Mister Mender. I'd certainly like to accommodate you this time, but, after all, there's your record. It's all on the books, you know. We can't ignore that."

"You mean Froody? And Honey Salkald? Why, they're both ..."

The manager interrupted. "Yes, I know, Mister Mender, I know. You took those two children and the collateral seemed all right at the time, but Froody's mother never came around. Neither did her daddy. Neither did Honey's dad. You promised, remember? But we've had to give you extensions every year since."

"And I think there's still time. Look at Honey's grand-dad. Look how well he shaped up before he died."

"Grandparents don't count, Mister Mender. I'm sorry. No, you've defaulted twice so we can't fill any new requests."

"But you can't refuse me like this. You know I would never come here like this if I weren't serious. How else is there? If you refuse like this you cut me off. Don't you understand? I've been working on these new ones ever since Froody and Honey . . ."

"Yes, Mister Mender, I know. But what you don't seem to understand is there are new developments in this business. They haven't been tried out too carefully yet, but there are going to be changes in the collateral rate at least. We have to go easy for a while and watch our balance sheet pretty carefully, much as we'd like to help people like yourself. What's troubling me is I'm the man in charge here, always have been. You've dealt with me before, yet I can't let the children go as easily as we used to. Those are orders. But I know what I'm doing to you. You old-timers have put me in a difficult position. And in your particular case, we thought you'd pretty well given up after you lapsed on Froody and Honey."

"But I'm old. You know better than to talk to me about changes. I know what you're talking about and all that jiggery-pokery makes me sick. Make you fellows mighty weary in a while, you mark my words. Collateral, lapses. That's all stuff. I'm eighty-seven years old. There's not much time left. I only need three children and you've got to give them to me."

The manager's face was troubled and firm. He followed Mr. Mender to the door. They stepped into the sun-baked street together. Slowly, for Mr. Mender's legs had gone stiff and old, they walked down the main street to the town line where the concession road began.

"I hope you understand my position here, Mister Mender. I'm only in charge of a local branch. If I were at head office I'm sure something could be arranged. Lord knows I'd like to help, because I think you are on the right track."

Old Johnson Mender made little throat-clearing noises and kept on walking to where the sidewalk ended and the eighth concession began.

"Would you care to tell me who the cases are, Mister Mender?"

"Yes. I'll tell you who they are, mister wise man. I'll tell you. Come over here and sit down. I'll tell you."

So the manager and Mr. Mender sat down in the dry grass by the side of the road. They were just outside the town. There was a new-cut barley field beside the road. A proud old elm in the fence bottom hung its big branches over them. Poplars lined both sides of the concession that narrowed straight into the township – reaching-up poplars, up to the sky. The manager's glasses glinted coldly in the warm sun.

While he listened, the manager thought of what was happening at that very moment. My world, he thought, is that field of barley there, long cleared of stumps, ploughed and cultivated, sown to barley and clover last spring, carefully harvested, stooked and threshed, and the clover left to get a root-hold for the winter. All order, all order, the manager thought. But his world is this long grass and weeds that grow thick-stemmed and too tough to destroy along the road where people go, up and down the road, close beside that.

"The first one, mister wise man, is my son, Tom. He's a fool. He's my son and a fool. He's down there right now at his house below the hill, sitting on the porch and rocking. And all he has inside him is 'This is my little farm. That's my barn and my root house and those are my mulberry trees and those are my chickens. I haven't missed a Sunday at church in twelve years. I get along good with my neighbours because I mind my own business. I don't owe anybody any money. That makes me a fortunate man!' And that's all he has to say to himself, mister wise man. What was it that stopped him there? He's fifty-five now, so I'm sure you'd get back the child I'd send there. Look, get this through your head. He's my son. He doesn't want to know who I am. He's afraid: so all I am is his father. That's good for some folks, but my son, he needs to know someone like me. Nothing bad would happen. Worse than that, he doesn't know who his wife is. Never once has he ever tried to get through to either of us.

"Kith, that's his wife, she came to me not so long ago, stern and proud, trying to hide it, not wanting to break down and wanting to, all at the same time. She did, and I tell you it's not good for an old man to be full of pity only. Not good."

The old man stopped to remember. He twisted a pigweed out by the root. It was red, covered with clay. The leaves would wilt by the time the two men were ready to leave.

"What kind of a life is that? Him proud-bound and dying in himself – and with a lonely wife. There are other things.

"I can see one of the children you could give me sitting on his shoulder, tugging at his ear and lifting up his eyelids and kicking him where his heart is to make it go. Imagine that heart going for the first time. It'd hurt at first and be a puzzle, but he'd come around.

"Then I got to send one to young Mordy MacDonald yonder. I tell you, mister wise man, Mordy is too proud. He's arrogant. Know what that word means? Arrogance is a sin and I've got to stop it.

"What makes a no-special-account family think it's got to lord and mister it and look down the nose on other people, like the MacDonalds've been doing since they first came here?

"What Mordy doesn't get is the juice that's in him is the same as the juice that's in everybody else. He bleeds when he's cut. He has a three-holer like everybody else. He puts his thumb down on the haft of the fork to get at his peas.

"Mordy's daddy started it all. Thinking he was too good for this country. He came here with nothing, like everybody else's daddy. There's no room now for what that old man did to Mordy.

"There's Mordy in his yard, looking up from filling the cow trough. He sees Swifts' barn next farm up. He sees Alex Thompson's barn across the road. He thinks they may have just as good barns as his, they may take off just as good crops as he does, but they haven't got the name.

"See what I'm driving at? Mordy's kids want to play with the Swifts. They want to buck-buck, how many fingers up at school in recess time, but Mordy'd skin them once he found out. They're getting too old for school now. Pretty soon they'll decide Mordy's all right. I got to catch them before that happens.

"You think this is all a lot of talk, mister wise man?" The old man mopped his face with his polka-dot handkerchief. His breath was coming faster.

"Now, Mister Mender, don't say that. You know better. I understand." Somehow the manager's face didn't appear as mean or troubled out here in the township as it did in town. He was where he wanted to belong: out among the living, but swallowed up. The long twitch-grass swam around his vision.

And, somehow, old Johnson Mender's eyes got all washed out. They halted in their moves from the horizon to the barley field to the manager's face and back again, halting and slow they were. The pigweed he'd pulled was already wilting in the sun.

"Go on, Mister Mender."

"The best thing for Mordy would be for him to be lifted up away from his farm with his head turned away from his name on the mail box. A child from your place could show him his neighbours. He'd come down and get to know Alex and the Swifts. One day he might cry inside over a little thing like shaking hands."

Something of the old man's fierceness came back to him; but whenever the sun winked on the wispy metal frames of the manager's glasses, Mr. Mender felt pity for the manager too, but mostly regret because it was in the manager's hands to do something for the almost blind. And when the old man started to speak again, the resentment of the manager was gone from his voice. He stopped calling him mister wise man. It was as though the old man's thoughts were now being put into his throat, into the words, by the unexpected excitement of dreaming out loud.

"Yes, that minister is almost blind. I was going to use the third one for the minister at the river church. Poor man. His softball league. Monthly reports. Marrying and burying. His balance sheet. Social services. He can't remember what was in him when he first started preaching. Nowadays when he gets together with the church wardens, all he can think about is he isn't making much money. He's never told anybody, but he'd like a church in the city. In the city. If he only knew he was here among his people.

"The other day his wife asked him if he'd let her have some extra money because she wanted a new hat to wear at the presbytery meeting in town. He didn't even see what the hat was. He didn't hear what his wife was saying. An easy thing like that. He gave her the money and she got the hat. Does he call that social service?

"And his sermons. You'd think he never heard of mothers or fathers, living or loving. They were what was in him when he first started preaching. They're not in him now. He hasn't preached a sermon in six years. We sit in our pews every Sunday but Sundays might as well be Saturdays or Thursdays. I thought sure he'd have heard his wife when she asked for money for a new hat.

"Boy, think of it. A child from your place at a Sunday morning christening. Right in the minister's arms. Looking up at him with eyes that say what needs to be said. You know that, don't you? You know I'm right. You know it'd work and you know you'd get the child back."

Excited inside, the manager nodded. He took his glasses off and for a second his sun-beat face was broken and eager. His fingers worked at the creases in his trousers as though he would jump up and start back to town. Instead he put his glasses back on.

"Why did you default on Froody and Honey, Mister Mender? I want to let you have the children, but I can't."

Mr. Mender pushed himself over and up to his feet. He walked in the weeds beside the road out into the township. The poplars, whispering and comforting, passed him on, one to another, into the country, towards the lake.

The manager stayed sitting by the side of the road. The disorderly weeds were big, green, swimming big in the corners of his sight. A stomach feeling in him was the fear that he was what made Mr. Mender dwindle so small as he walked away. He moved his eyes from near to far to keep the old man in sight, but the poplars kept passing the old man along from one to the next and on.

And the twitch-grass, yellowy green and hard to kill, the nodding Queen Anne's lace, the blue devil, up over all, the roadside life filled his sight. All that was left was the road out into the township. The road that went back into town too. He got up and turned.

Where the base-line road crosses the eighth concession, there are two rural delivery boxes, one for Mr. Mender and the other for his son, Tom. This was where Kith found her father-in-law when she came up the hill for the mail. He was slumped against the anchor post behind the mail boxes. She ran back down the hill, calling for Tom.

Tom came and carried his father down the hill, under the mulberry trees that shaded the porch, then up on the porch to the horsehair sofa. He laid him down.

"I'll phone for Doctor Fletcher," Tom said; "loosen his shirt and swab his face."

Kith was left alone with old Johnson Mender. Before he opened his eyes, he considered the warm old smell of ripe mulberries. He opened his eyes and saw Tom was not there.

"Kith," he whispered, "I was going to do something about Tom. Can't now. You'd have seen it right away. It would have made you glad. Everything would have worked out. Could've changed him, but they wouldn't let me. Too late now.

"I had a plan, Kithy. Wonderful plan. Three little children. One takes a little run and a hop, floating easily down here right under the porch roof one afternoon, just an instant. But enough. Another glides into Mordy's yard. Another, shining clean and humming, looks up at the minister at the christening next Sunday morning. Too late now. They wouldn't let me."

His voice and his eyes became washed-out whispers. Kith could feel him strain for every breath. She heard Tom's footsteps in the house. She bent over the old man quickly.

"Wait, Daddy, wait," she spoke in his ear, "don't go. What children? What do you mean? What do the children mean?"

TEN

The commonplace

1st person?

THE GREY SNOWS OF SPRING lay melting in the shallow ditches by the roads in the township. The town was without colour and we were relieved that winter was over. It was the time of year when adult faces were sallow and when children couldn't imagine a longer time than the three months until the end of school.

That was when the Sunbird family arrived in town.

There was talk about them. Some people said they were "holy rollers." The deputy reeve said they were gypsies and ought to be run out of town.

They set up housekeeping in the Langmaid House, but never told old Mr. Langmaid about this arrangement. The Langmaid House was an empty hotel across the street and a little down from the Queen's. Once it had style – real style. There was a long mahogany bar with a mirror behind it. There was a big oil painting above the mirror, maybe nine feet long, but it was covered with burlap and none of us ever saw it. Honey Salkald claimed it was a picture of a fat naked lady with pigeons and clouds. There was a crystal chandelier in the hall, like the one the Kennedys got for the Queen's that time, and real gilt mirrors all around what used to be the dining-room. Double doors with small panes of purple glass led out of the hotel to the street and there was a porte cochère with a hitching-post and a granite step for when there were carriages.

The only way to put it is the Sunbirds were led by Ingram Sunbird. He was dark with hairy big arms. He roared a lot at his family. They got off the noon train one day, trooped down the street behind old Ingram, and marched straight into the Langmaid House. Somebody told Mister Langmaid, but he was too old to do anything about it.

For a week there was a lot of banging and sawing going on inside the hotel during daylight. Nights they seemed to sing and laugh a lot. When the cardboard crates arrived from the chick hatchery near the city, we knew the Sunbirds were going to raise chicks and sell them for a living.

There were eighteen of them all together. There was Ingram, the only one who had business dealings with the town people. He bought things at the hardware store – things you'd expect they'd need to fix up the hotel. He paid cash. He paid cash for feed for the chicks. He paid cash for groceries every Saturday at Mills's. He dealt quiet all the time, but a little firm as though daring somebody to ask him about his family.

Jemima Sunbird was olive-skinned and noisy like her husband, and she had a knowing look like his, too. There were four more adult Sunbirds, but nobody ever found out just exactly who they were. They were dark like Jemima and Ingram, and maybe a few years younger. It seemed like a lot of people to be raising chicks for sale in a town the size of ours.

The rest of them were children. Four of them, we found out, were Ingram's and Jemima's. They were Van, Robert, Lillian and Bertram. The other eight children we never did figure out, who their parents were, or anything.

Froody got to be friends with Lillian Sunbird at high school, as close friends as was possible. They were about the same age. Froody did it by being able to talk to anybody about nearly anything. She was like that. Froody could talk easily about her parents and brothers and even lip them if she had a mind to; but Lillian never dared speak to anybody about her family.

Lillian acted the same over Froody and Honey Salkald walking home from school together.

"It's nothing, Lil," Froody said. "He likes it. I don't mind. Nothing could happen, for heaven's sake. Not with Honey, anyway."

"My dad'd kill me if it was me," Lillian said.

The school year got on to the long, warm days and Lillian fitted in better with the rest of them. So did her brother, Bertram, except Bertram would start walking towards you quietly if you ever called him Bert or Bertie. Couple of the fellows tried it once and Honey had to step between them.

By the time school opened again in September, the Sunbird family was accepted as permanent in the town, but they had no friends. Bertram and Lillian were the connection with us in town.

School opened and the threshing season was under way in the township. Honey Salkald and Bertram Sunbird were the spike-pitchers at most of the threshings that year. Spike-pitching is the steadiest job at a threshing. You spend the whole day in the fields, loading the wagons. You get no relief, because, while you load one wagon, another one has been unloaded into the separator. There's always an empty wagon waiting to load. Sixteen wagons to load in the forenoon is ordinary for two good men.

Under the hot September sun, spike-pitching stiffens the fingers into curved, calloused claws. Your back feels like the sound of cicadas on a hot day on the dunes. By nightfall, you're not thinking of anything or anybody, least of all yourself.

One night, after the thresher let go the quitting whistle and before dinner was on, Honey and Bertram sat in the cool of the barn shade.

"I feel pretty good," Bertram said.

"How many did you pitch on?"

"Fourteen and part of two others, I think."

"And you feel pretty good?"

"Sure."

"Let's see your hands."

Bertram held them out. The great callus pads were yellow in the centre and faded out to pink on the edges. Dust clung to the hairs on his wrists. They were strong hands.

"I think I could beat my dad any day now," Bertram said.

"At what?"

"Wrestling."

"You wrestle with him much?"

"Never."

"What made you think of it now?"

"Because it's time I did, that's all."

The bell for dinner rang and the two young men walked out of the shade of the barn, across the yard, into the house. They had been friends in the fields, but not any more.

It must have been Indian summer when the four of them – Lillian and Bertram Sunbird, Froody and Honey – went for a picnic down the river valley where the banks are high and cut sharply away.

It was a Saturday afternoon. Froody and Lillian walked ahead together, Froody doing all of the talking, telling Lil about the people in each farmhouse as they passed it. Honey and Bertram carried the baskets and did not want to speak to each other all the way down the concession road and across the fields to the edge of the river valley. They agreed on a place to spread the blanket at the top of the high clay bank that fell away down to the sluggish old river below.

From there they could look west and see the tops of the black green cedars that grow this way from the sand dunes on the lake shore. They could look east across the river valley and see familiar farm buildings. Down in the river bed they could see the trails made by horses and cattle. They led to the river and disappeared. On the other side of the river was a flat area, sandy, with scrub cedars scattered around.

When the four sat down on the ground by the blanket with the food all laid out, Lillian didn't seem interested in what Froody or Honey said about the countryside and the people. Bertram seemed confident and would have spoken freely to Honey if he and Honey were alone.

The sky was warm. There was lots of food. Froody and Honey were contented in their township; but out in the country, Lillian and Bertram felt friendless. At least it could be lost in town. They ate quietly, the four of them. Lillian was grave. Froody was a little proud because she had prepared the picnic lunch. The familiarity of it all was enough for Honey. It was all his.

"Let's talk about something important," Froody said.

✗ "War is hell, peace is wonderful, life is real, death is certain. Something like that?" Honey's eyes were on Froody's neck.

"No. About loving. About love."

Lillian and Honey, separately, were uncomfortable. They looked down at the grass beside them. Froody was frightened because she realized young people talking about love was wrong and shouldn't happen. She wanted to try anyway, even though it might end the picnic.

"What do you want us to say?" Honey asked.

"How does it begin?" Froody didn't dare clear her throat or cough. Her question was a whisper.

"It begins in the eyes," Bertram said.

"Then what?"

"It spreads to the mind."

"No. Love is a chance. There's no telling when it begins."

"And you've got to see someone."

"Yes. And look at all the people you see that you don't love."

"Somebody has to say something."

"Exactly. That's why it's all chance."

"And when the chance comes it begins in the eyes and spreads to the mind and if you are aware you are careful because it is new and you keep it secret," Bertram said.

"It can be disappointing too. Very quickly," Lillian said.

"Quickly?"

"It depends on how soon is the first kiss."

"Oh yes," excited, Froody spoke, "that's always a disappointment I guess. So funny."

"How many first kisses have you been on?" Honey asked.

"Be serious, Honey."

"Probably is disappointing. The kiss itself. But the idea isn't, is it?"

"Kissing got anything to do with love?"

"It begins with the eyes and spreads to the mind and it's a chance and it begins in secret. The first kiss is important because it is the idea of taking from each other. Birds feed their young by placing the food in their beaks." Bertram was patient.

"Why disappointing?"

"Oh, boys are so clumsy."

"And girls are so stiff."

"You soon get over it."

"And love stops because of the commonplace," Bertram said.

"What's that?"

"What's what?"

"Commonplace."

"Kissing for what it does to the blood."

They stopped then. Froody, Honey and Lillian were disappointed. The excitement that only the four of them could create, doing that, was gone. It was Bertram's fault. They all knew it.

"Indian summer," Honey said.

"Time for moving." Lillian looked nervously at her brother.

"Notice the grasshoppers are all gone."

"That's right."

"Nothing for birds to eat soon."

They couldn't keep the talk going. The strain on Lillian and on Honey was easy to see because they were not interested in each other. They squirmed around and sat on the edge of the bank. The steep clay fell away in ripples. It was clean and indifferent. The water away below wasn't dangerous.

Suddenly, for he was very strong, Bertram stood up and lifted Froody in his arms, all in one motion. Honey knew how strong Bertram was and he felt weak.

There was a way down the high bank to the flat lands below, to where the cedar clumps were. It was along the top of the bank for a way, to the rail fence where there was a crude stile. Here there was a grassy lane cut out of the side of the bank in a gentle slope for maybe forty rods. At the bottom, little tracks were worn in the clay by the farm animals on their way to the river. At that time of year it was easy to step across stones in the river and get to the other side.

Bertram stood up, then, with Froody in his arms. Honey's first feeling was weakness because he knew how strong Bertram was. He had seen the yellow callus pads and the dusty hair on his wrists. When Bertram started walking away from the blanket where the food was spread and where Honey and Lillian sat, Honey was filled with horror because he was now so small and the sky seemed far off. There was nothing to hold to. Lillian was there, not looking, only staring down the clay bank.

Bertram walked easily. The sun was warm. He didn't look at Froody's face. He looked straight ahead. Froody looked hard at his face, hoping to make him bend his head so she could meet his eyes. He walked along and watched where he was going. Honey thought he walked quietly and didn't know where he was going.

Bertram climbed over the stile with Froody in his arms. Then he was on the sloping road down to the flats. At first, Honey could see all of Bertram, his legs moving away, Froody in her red dress in his arms, his head. Gradually, for he walked slowly, his legs went out of sight. Then a clump of choke-cherry trees came between them. Then all Honey could see was Bertram's head and flashes of Froody's dress now and then. Then they were out of sight for a while and the air was still. At the bottom of the long hill, they appeared again. They were tiny. The silence weakened Honey and his head hung so his chin was pressed against his breastbone. He didn't seem to be watching Bertram and Froody at all. He couldn't hear their steps on the sandy soil of the river flat-land. He wanted to hear. He didn't know if they were speaking. He wanted to know if Froody was frightened.

They were by the river now. Bertram walked along the water's edge until he found a shallow place where the rocks were big and firm. He stepped across them and didn't miss. He was graceful. On the far side of the river now, they were beyond Honey's reach. He could look over at Lillian now when he wasn't looking helplessly down on them from a high distance. They disappeared behind a cedar clump and appeared again closer to the centre part of the flat-land.

Bertram didn't walk in a straight line, but walked easily around the cedar clumps, until he came to a clear area that was surrounded by bushes that grew in the shape of a horse-shoe. He let Froody down. He took the two ribbons from her hair and hung them up in the branches of a bush. Then he took her hat and placed it on another branch. He took off his tie and hat and put them on branches. He took out his hand-kerchief and hung it up. The little bits of cloth fluttered in a breeze that Honey couldn't feel up on the river bank, and the horror of it hurt his stomach.

Bertram stood before Froody in the little clear area. He

took her hands in his and they walked sideways around the cleared area. Then they walked sideways in the other direction, still holding hands.

Gradually the pace of their sedate step was quickened and Honey realized it was a kind of dance. He couldn't hear from that distance, but he thought he heard, now and then, Bertram's voice singing.

They were skipping lightly round in a circle by now, and Froody's dress flared out. There seemed to be no weight to her at all.

She was up in his arms again and he walked out of the flatland in the bushy trees that grew on the far side of the river. They had disappeared.

The tears came easy on Honey's face and he had no strength in his hands to wipe at them. He let them come. He didn't sniffle. His shoulders didn't hump up. The tears came and he didn't stop them.

Day by day the skies grew duller. The leaves fell. Dust flew in the empty streets of town. The threshings were over. Honey thought there was no reason to see Froody again. He arranged to pass the Langmaid House as often as he could on Saturday nights when he was in town.

He tried to put out of his mind the events that were there, but he couldn't. Sometimes, say when he was walking from Geddes's to Mills's, he looked into Weaver's barber shop, saw what he used to like in there and felt he would like to go in again. Instead he walked on to the Langmaid House and stood, cold, under the porte cochère. The children were noisy inside and there seemed a lot of them.

One Saturday night he stood in the doorway with Bertram, Ingram and Jemima, uncomfortable, not able to say much, when a child came running along the street.

"Mommy, mommy, we saw fifty blackbirds in a field."

Ingram and Jemima looked at each other. Honey stood smiling hopefully at the child. Bertram started to turn away, to go into the hotel.

"Look at him skulk away now he knows he can't do it this year." Ingram snorted at Bertram.

"You won't escape. There's another year. I'll wait," Bertram said.

There was nothing to be said among them now. Honey was relieved to get away from them and he went down the street looking for Froody to tell her what he knew. He found her with Aunt Cress in talking with Mr. Geddes.

Froody turned towards him as he came in the door. Her face was plain. Aunt Cress and Mr. Geddes moved down the store a little.

"All he did was sing and dance around with me a little, Honey. Bertram, he's very much older than you and me. Very much older." She smiled hopefully to Honey.

The Sunbirds, all of them, left that night and a cold snow blew down from the north the following morning.

ELEVEN

The way back

S HE LAY BIG AND comfortable with Dan inside her, the familiar patchwork quilt over her knees. When the pains started once more it would be time for her husband to go for the doctor.

Thin and sharp-faced, he sat on the cedar chest at the foot of the bed. He pushed out a little with his lower lip: a new habit he had gotten into to try and get a knowing and confident look that he wanted. She didn't like it when he did this, but never spoke about it. She connected the pouting lip with his endless gossip about the people in the axe-handle factory.

When she was a girl at home – she thought of it just that moment – there was no such talking about business at the supper table. So she didn't permit it in her house after she got married.

But it was an effort for him to keep up the innocent flow of talk and planning. It was easier for him to come home nights and talk about the people he worked with: sort of flow them on into his life at home.

The pains started coming. He looked at her, his eyebrows raised.

"Yes. Go now, go now," she whispered.

He got up and she made a motion with her hand. He turned. He knew what she wanted.

"You'll get the grinder man too?" she pleaded. He frowned as he shook his head.

"Please? This last time?"

He left. He left the door open. She heard his steps on the porch, along the cement walk, on the sidewalk of the street, under the oaks leading to the main street.

She didn't know whether the grinder man would be standing outside the house for this birth. He had been there for the other two children. Both times before, her husband had gone for the grinder man when he went for the doctor.

She knew that all you had to do to get the grinder man was stand on Doc Fletcher's back stoop and call for him. He'd show up in a minute.

There'd be no grinder man this time. Just Doc Fletcher.

People in town never considered the possibility of a birth-giving without the familiar old figure standing on the walk outside the house. Without ever thinking twice about it, people knew a woman's time had come as soon as they saw the old man outside her house. There he'd be: a gnarled, brown old man, his back curved, standing still, his sharpening machine down on the walk in front of him. It was his living.

So this day, the people saw Doc Fletcher's horse and buggy tied up outside, but no grinder man. Somebody must be sick, they thought at first. But it dawned on them with terror for the unborn and with shame for the father: this birth was to happen without the grinder man.

So Dan was born. A healthy gurgling child he was. But the people were ashamed for his father and were full of pity for his mother. She could say nothing, she couldn't defend or ignore. She was ashamed too.

Looking at his third and last child for the first time, Dan's father was sharply aware of the shame and sympathy, and pressed his back molars down hard and shoved out his lower lip that way he had.

He paid. There was the time Dan turned four years old. His shaking old aunt in New York sent him a blown ostrich egg for a birthday present. In another family it would have become a private treasure to be looked at and held and wondered at. Dan did his best to keep his father from enjoying it. He kept it carefully wrapped in cotton batting in an old jewellery box and hid the box under the bed.

Then there was the dead June bug hanging by a thread on the bedroom wall. Dan kept it alive in a match-box for a few days. When the bug died, he hung it by a piece of silk thread so it was a few inches from his head when he lay in bed. First his father asked in a friendly way what it meant and Dan screamed. Then his father wanted it taken down and Dan screamed louder and almost got sick.

A boy grows up that way, it's no wonder his father starts worrying over the grinder man.

It was a May day when things were quiet and Dan was home from school for lunch. He played a secret game of buck-buck, how many fingers up, bouncing gently on his chair at the table and making whispered grunting noises. His father sat thin and isolated, chips of hickory in his hair. His mother, placid and hopeful, served the meal efficiently.

The sound of the grinder man's bell was heard far off, coming from maybe three streets over, through the trees, over the houses, into this window. His mother sat up and smiled. He noticed she turned her head a little as though to hear every sound of the bell. His father frowned. He noticed that too. Dan didn't know what to do. He knew that the kids would be running out of their houses now, down this street, across that side street, looking up and down for the grinder man. He did it once himself, but he would never do it again. Not after what happened.

He got up from the table slowly, pushed his chair back in carefully, and went out the back door. The sound of the grinder man's bell was loud. He wanted to go to it.

"That's the grinder man's bell," his mother said.

"I know, I know," his father said.

"Why doesn't Dan run to it, the way we used to, I wonder?"

"You know why. What do you ask for? It's ridiculous."

"All the other kids are running over. Dan's still out in the back yard."

"Listen. I'll take that kid out of school and put him to work if you don't shut up. Grinder man. Shut up."

"Work?"

"Yes, work. Work's what matters nowadays. Nothing else. Stuff like that grinder man gives me the pip. He's nothing better than a bogeyman women are scared of."

"But he's not for the women," she cried softly. "Women aren't frightened of him. They like him. He's for the men, for the fathers. It's the fathers that benefit. You know that."

He knew she was right by what their parents had told them, but it was a story, mystery, something concealed, a feeling. That was bad. He got up and banged his chair into place and went out the front door quickly. She was left crying in shame and sympathy.

Dan watched his father go down the street and heard the sound of the bell grow louder and louder from the other direction. The old man was coming on this street.

Crouched in the bushes waiting, Dan knew that it was the grinder man that had somehow caused the anger between his mother and father, but he didn't think about it for long. He wished he could go to the old man with the other kids. He saw them walking and skipping along behind and around him.

Dan couldn't go with them because of his father. He knew.

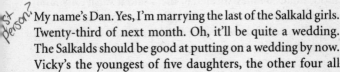

My name's Dan. Yes, I'm marrying the last of the Salkald girls. Twenty-third of next month. Oh, it'll be quite a wedding. The Salkalds should be good at putting on a wedding by now. Vicky's the youngest of five daughters, the other four all married. It'll be in their rose garden, with a trellis of roses behind the preacher and two nieces of mine carrying wicker baskets of roses and two of Vicky's nephews in sailor suits. Everybody'll be there, sitting on chairs borrowed from the Orange Lodge and everything'll go smoothly, even the photograph after it's over.

I met her at the factory of course. Where else could I meet her? Don't you know who I am? I'm the only man in this town born without the grinder man standing outside the day I was born. It was no oversight. My old man could have afforded it, all right. He just decided it didn't mean anything and he was bound he'd try it once. It broke my mother's heart. Didn't do me any good either. Thing like that, if you don't have a feeling for it, it'll separate you from the kids in school. It doesn't matter if your family's one of the oldest in town. You just don't live it down.

For a long time I thought my old man had the right idea. The grinder man was an old-fashioned idea. Times were changing. There had to be a break some time. He did it. When I was a kid I was kind of proud of him. Proud. Now I'm old enough and I'm ashamed of him, the way my mother is, the way my brothers are. I feel sorry for them and him the way everybody in town does. It wasn't a question of fashion or times changing.

Honey Salkald will be my brother-in-law. That makes me proud. Honey's a good man. He won't have anything to do with me, though. Last Saturday night we were in Mac's office, sitting around kidding Mac about his map with all the pins in it and about the money he makes peddling insurance, the way we always do Saturday nights, and Honey and me, we had it out finally. Honey sneered at me. I said it wasn't my fault, but that didn't matter. Honey's right to sneer. I should get out of town as soon as we're married, but I can't leave. It's all I know. If only there was a place for me. A connection.

I remember when I was just a kid playing with the others, nice as you please, when there was the sound of the grinder man's bell, the only sound on a lazy summer day, coming from away off. We all jumped and ran for it as fast as we could go. But as soon as we caught up with him, the others laughed at me and told me to go on home, the grinder man'd have nothing to do with me.

You know, I was sixteen years old before I found out. I heard what everybody else knew at a garden party down at the river church. There were two girls from town there. I sat beside one in particular during dinner and her skin was clear and she smiled at me when I looked at her and we talked and got along first rate. We kind of kept together after dinner. We watched the softball game together, sometimes standing a little apart pretending not to be together when any of our relatives walked near. Her girl friend sort of hung around.

When it got dark, the gas lamps were lit on the stage back of the church. The stage was really John Reid's wagon rack. They used it for a stage because it was tongue-and-groove hardwood and smooth from all the loads of hay and grain that had rubbed it for ten years. This girl and her girl friend and I went with the crowd from the ball park across the road to the church. Most all of the good seats were taken, but there was a sleigh tipped up on its side against the drive shed and a bunch of us sat on it and had a good view of the stage.

She decided to sit with her girl friend, so I was kind of left out, but I hung around and managed to sit right behind her only a little up. The programme got started and everybody was watching the stage except me. I was thinking about her the way a boy would and wondering what I could get away with. I moved closer to her, willing her to do what I wanted her to do. I spread my knees apart and put my hands down between my knees. Then, slowly, as the programme went on, I moved my hands closer to her until I touched her back.

Nothing happened. I made my hands move more around on her sides and felt the softness there. And she didn't move at all. I knew she was a quiet one and I knew she would come with me if I dared ask. Then the programme was over and the violinist and some baritone from up country led in "God Save the Queen" and there was a lot of talking and laughing. The girl friend turned around and caught me with my hands where they shouldn't have been. She whispered all about me to the girl I wanted. I heard then what everybody else knew and I knew and I walked all the way home and I was late and my father was mad at me and I didn't care.

Shortly after that I met Victoria Salkald. Don't you see? I had to marry a girl from the country. It couldn't be one from town. They all knew. I told Vicky all about it, but it didn't bother her somehow.

On the Sunday she said she would marry me, I asked her what her family thought about it. She said it didn't matter what her family thought as long as her grandfather was around. I never knew the old blister had it over the family the way he did. I asked Vicky what she meant.

"You mean about the way you were born?"

"Of course."

"Oh, it came up at Sunday dinner once when I told them that I thought you would be asking me to marry you."

"What happened?"

"Grandma got mad and left the table. Granfer made her come back and behave. Granfer kept eating away, looked at me now and then. Finally he said there is always hope of return. That was the end of it."

Things are working out too smoothly. I guess that's not a thing to say less than a month before your wedding day, but it's a fact. Vicky's happy. I'm happy. My mother's happy. And my old man has it in his head that this all proves something. The other night when I showed him the wedding ring he said to me flatly, "You worked out all right after all, eh?"

"What do you mean?"

"Oh, just that you're getting married to a nice girl and all."

"No thanks to you."

"I mean some people figure you got off to a bad start," he said lightly. "It looks now as though maybe you didn't."

Then I saw the confidence in him was a November hoar frost that disappears in the heat of the day. I left him and thought of going to my mother, but knew that would be warm and useless and this terrible undertone of regret. I couldn't face it.

As I went down the street it dawned on me where my father's confidence came from. His father would have seen to it that the grinder man was outside the day my father was born. So my father had been given the right to a serene life, and to things I can't speak of.

I wanted to know how it had happened. Surely my grand-father had planned it differently. But we had experienced the contempt and shame of the others. I didn't know how it had happened. My father was the end and I was the beginning.

"I guess I'll wait until after the week-end to wean the baby," Victoria said, and the word was there in front of Dan so he could think of nothing else and he got out of the house and down the street to be alone with the word and the act and to wonder what to do.

He avoided the old man who sat under the willow tree by the pond because the old man knew and his pity would be too real. He avoided the high school and he avoided the Seaton place and walked out the township road to where it was unfamiliar.

He thought of it all and tried to see Victoria the way she was, but couldn't. He tried to feel the way of his life from the time he first learned about the grinder man, but couldn't. He wondered when he last saw the grinder man, but it didn't matter because the figure of him was there and

Dan considered a new reason for the old man: to let the mother and the father acknowledge the child as an adult at the right time. So it wasn't exactly for the fathers, the way his mother always said. It was for mothers and fathers, and Dan needed a way back. Victoria's father said there was hope of return. He had hope but Dan hadn't, so Dan was tired and isolated and wanting to believe in Victoria's father.

If something would only come to him, he hoped on his way back home, a little ashamed for having run from the house at the sound of the word. Why should it bother him now? He had heard it before, had seen the act twice before. This was the third weaning. There was nothing unusual about it. Yes. This was the last. That was it. The last weaning. Where is the hope of return now, Mister Salkald?

He came home at last and saw there was a light in the parlour and knew Victoria was there, and he loved her, but he went in by the back door, quietly, knowing she heard, but not wanting her to see him the way he was. He sat down at the bare table and his head felt tired and he said over to himself the few ideas he wanted to hold. The grinder man is there, outside the door to a birth-giving so that the father and the child can love. He is there so that the father and the mother will assert the child's adulthood at the right times. He wasn't there when I was born, Dan thought, so I see the difference between the life of my father and the life of the heart. I want the life of the heart and Mister Salkald says there is hope, there is a way back. This is the connection.

He sat up straight in the red kitchen chair and his knee bumped the table leg, and the knives, forks and spoons in the drawer rattled against each other. Victoria came in the kitchen then and he wondered if it was wrong to think about hating her. She led him to the bedroom. They undressed and went to bed.

Early in the morning, he went into the basement and got his hatchet, his draw-knife, his axe and the rusty old scythe that belonged to Mr. Salkald, Victoria's father. The familiarity and the reality of them all soothed him and he planned confidently what he was going to do. He placed them carefully in the grass by the side door. Then, while Victoria went, with the baby, down the street to shop, he cleared the kitchen table drawer of the paring knives, the long butcher knife, the kitchen scissors, and he remembered to get the scissors from her sewing basket.

Standing on the sidewalk, with some of them in his hands and the others in the grass, he waited for the grinder man.

When Victoria came home, Dan was not around. The hatchet, the axe, the blade of the scythe, the two pairs of scissors, the draw-knife, all her kitchen knives, all sharpened, were on the kitchen table.

She knew. If she had not known, she would have left Dan that day and gone to the farm to live with her brother, for good. But she knew. She had always known. She had remembered what her grandfather had said. She hoped this was the way.

She picked up the draw-knife and noticed the way the light flashed on the newly sharpened surface. So he had been around.

This was Granfer's knife, she thought. He had made shingles with it and rough-shaped wheel spokes and axe handles with it. It had been his knife. Maybe this was the way. And that was Granfer's scythe, too. She saw his tall figure in memory, moving slowly along the fence by the roadside, the scythe swinging in rhythm, and she remembered the sound of the seeuhree-seeuhruh of the stone on the blade of the scythe as Granfer sharpened it. Maybe this was the way.

She heated the gruel on the back of the stove and was impatient to get on with it. She put a little of the gruel in a bowl on a tray and moved with it out of the kitchen door towards the bedroom where the baby was. As she left the kitchen, Dan came in from the yard and saw that the scythe blade was missing from the kitchen table and regretted his wonder about hating Victoria, then he was impatient too.

The baby cried a lot and the gruel was on his face, and Victoria was kind with him. She waited for him to want it. She wished that she could be near a window so she could see out on the street. She wondered where Dan was. The baby cried and the tears mixed with the gruel and Victoria looked under the bed over and over again to make sure she had really put the shining blade there.

Then the baby took a few spoonfuls of the gruel and managed it very easily. She set the bowl aside and hurried out to the kitchen were Dan was. They smiled to each other. They went out the front door and onto the porch and looked down the street. Then they heard the bell and the grinder man walked up their street and stopped on their path and put his grinding machine down. He fiddled with the leather carrying-strap, put his hands in his pockets, looked up at them at last and smiled back.

Afterword

BY BONNIE BURNARD

Good fiction writers make the move: they have the desire and the confidence and the skill to go *inside* an *other*. This is the thing we cannot do in our real lives, although, knowing that we cannot, we still persist, we make attempts. A good literary story confirms what we suspect or, perhaps more accurately, what we want to be true: it is worth our every effort.

In *The Kissing Man*, George Elliott assumes a profoundly honest narrative intimacy. He does not struggle or fuss around; he goes *inside* his characters and stays there. Although the town and the rural area that surrounds it, the era in which these characters find themselves, and the conflicts among and between them are offered up with deliberation, with care for detail and emotional accuracy, intimacy itself, quiet, forgiving intimacy, seems to be the point.

Intimacy will teach you many things, the first of these being that loneliness is pervasive and natural to the human condition. Elliott seems to be interested equally in the chilling loneliness of his characters and in the mysteries of the outsiders who either live among them or come to them and to their loneliness from that great unknown, another place.

The people who belong in and around this town are not weak or particularly dull-witted. Many of them have quite effectively made themselves immune to possibility, and this kind of refusal does require a kind of strength, a kind of energy, a kind of intelligence.

But it is the outsiders, who appear in the narrative as if from nowhere (like angels?) with their raw, clumsy courage, who bring the town and the characters and the stories to life. The outsiders possess (are possessed by?) both the ability to see things as they are and the compulsion to translate what they know, to speak directly. Anyone who has grown up in my part of southern Ontario and, yes, in many other places, will recognize this speaking directly as something very closely akin to the power of angels.

There is refusal in these stories, and there is risk.

The refusal of many of the characters to feel pleasure, to love, to relax a bit into life, is a collective response. This refusal could be understood as a side effect, a conditioned response to the living of a hard rural or small-town life. It is the stoic, nothing-will-surprise-me strength of people for whom basic survival must always be the first impetus, of people who have little energy left for nuance or joy. In these stories, nearly all the people work hard and their work is included in the telling of their stories as an ordinary, significant part of their days. They tend the dying and the newborn, cut hair, gather eggs, stook barley, renovate and manage hotels; they build barns, hew beams that show not a single mark of the broad axe. Their cold, limiting, stoic strength is an almost admirable defence against what they can too readily imagine. Perhaps we should not condemn it too easily.

But not even children are much loved in this place and time. Many of the fathers offer only an exhausted, brute stupidity, and the mothers do not yet have enough power to counter it. I am reminded here of something I used to see: the secretly offered consolations of powerless mothers, the treat slipped into a small hand, the quick, sly look that says, we can live through this, you and I. I am reminded that not long ago and not far away this was very common, and necessary.

In the absence of the luxury of love or its daily stand-in, simple, easy affection, and as a reward for their stolid endurance, Elliott's characters allow themselves set rituals of pleasure. Once a year, every year, there is a fall fair, then a ploughing match, then a carnival. These social rituals offer a kind of mass distraction which is both harmless and knowable, something to look forward to, some thing, some activity to help make the rough dullness of *now* disappear. Amazingly, for only a brief time (of course for only a brief time; excess cannot last long here), Allie's magical Saturday-night parties at the beautifully refurbished hotel offer a more refined, more delicate distraction. Daily, although not for everyone, there is the distraction of gossip. And it is the real thing, it is power-hungry gossip, not banter, not the men having a bit of fun up at the barbershop.

The refusal in these stories is collective and easily understood. Because the movement into cities has been relatively recent, many of us have memories or at least memories of stories of a harder life. But the attempts to defeat refusal, the risks, never arise collectively and they are often, perhaps for that very reason, singularly peculiar and odd. With the exception of the twins, Jacob and Esau, and this hardly counts as an exception because they are so connected (they cuddle together for warmth on the straw in the shed behind the hotel), the people who take the risks act alone and they act strangely. In the graveyard, the boy Honey takes his family's past into himself as he might take bread and wine. Jacob and Esau are orphans without protection for whom every action, every hope, is a risk. Doctor Fletcher, determinedly secretive, risks and receives the wrath of the townsmen whose lodge he will not join. Allie risks the potential humiliation attendant on the too large social gesture because she is so unashamedly placing herself in the path of hope, of pleasure and happiness. The kissing man, who sneaks around touching, holding, kissing selected lonely women, risks ridicule and likely physical reprisal from the rest of the men, who would not themselves touch these women any more than they would rape them. Finn, by believing in the possibility of trout and by leaving on "the one-twenty flag-down" (and is that not a marvellous combination of words?) to go out into the world alone, risks his entire, unknown future. The man who lived out loud risks the town's confident, rock-solid contempt: "We aren't talkers like you," Muncey says. In this time and place, talking, talking directly, trying to get some of what is inside outside, is known to be, at the very least, useless and, more often than not, dangerously foolish.

Elliott's outsiders do not become less alone as a result of the risks they take, but it seems to me they do become less lonely. Elliott might be suggesting that the solution to his characters' loneliness is not to be found in community, in bland belonging or simple joining, but in risk, in action, in *doing* precisely the thing that their loneliness prompts them to do. And it does not seem to matter much what it is they risk; any number of things will do the trick.

Some of the best characters here, the ones worth watching, are the ones who *know* or who are beginning to *know*. Elliott often uses this word. In the first story, old Mrs. Palson sits waiting to pounce with her *knowing*, taps on her window with a thimble (why is this so creepy?) to get Honey's attention. Doctor Fletcher says about the twins before they are born, not at all casually, "They'll be boys." Froody wants to know things: "Let's talk about something important. . . . About loving. About love." Allie, a married woman, knows which men in the town love her, hangs a crystal bead in her chandelier for each of these men as a sign to them that she does know (this has caused me to take a good long look at my own, more modest chandelier) and, later in the story, a much older Allie knows when these men are about to die, weeps for them (and each time, feeling the absence, she marks it, removes a crystal from the chandelier, asks her husband to take it away, to smash it). The old man who sits under the willow waiting for Finn knows about Finn's mother, about the trout. The kissing man in the title story has no other qualities at all, he simply knows and acts from that knowing.

I recognize many of the specific physical places in these stories because I have lived, briefly, in the town of Strathroy, Ontario, where Elliott himself once briefly lived. I have driven past the mill pond, the dam, the hotel, walked the main street, walked down over the springy plank bridge to the fair grounds. Strathroy is surely the inspiration for the particulars of this fiction, and the imaginative rendering of a place I can recognize gives me a kind of solid pleasure (the increasing strength of Canadian fiction, the transformation of my own place into fiction, is something I can no longer imagine living without). And there is pleasure too in Elliott's precisely built sentences, his control of cadence, his combinations, his soft foldings of words one into the other. And in the silence, recognizable and informative, which surrounds his people.

The kissing man's question, "Why is it that order of living, loving and loneliness?" is an astonishingly intimate, gentle question. In these stories, it is well and properly asked.